M M SKUTETZKI was born in Warsaw in 1981. He holds degrees from the University of Warsaw, University of Westminster and the Nottingham Trent University. His passions are books, history, art and travelling. He lives and works in London.

M M Skutetzki

SilverWood

Published in 2017 by SilverWood Books

SilverWood Books Ltd
14 Small Street, Bristol, BS1 1DE, United Kingdom
www.silverwoodbooks.co.uk

ISBN 978-1-78132-559-9 (paperback)
ISBN 978-1-78132-647-3 (ebook)

British Library Cataloguing in Publication Data
A CIP catalogue record for this book is available from
the British Library

Page design and typesetting by SilverWood Books
Printed on responsibly sourced paper

Life is its own journey,
presupposes its own change and movement,
and one tries to arrest them at one's eternal peril

Laurens van der Post

Contents

Simple Kindness

I had had enough; enough of sitting on my own in the house; enough of not knowing whether Tom, my partner of six years, had another affair. Paradoxically, that is why I was standing in Wardour Street in Soho on the eve of St Valentine's Day. I tried to get some kinky and rather rude card celebrating February the fourteenth, a card which would not be over the top and which would not show too much of love, too much of affection. Two months ago my world broke – Tom told me that he had had an affair. He did not deserve my usual loving card, my usual loving pathetic heart...

I got a card; really quite vulgar, not even funny, just obscene. At least I had something for the day what would tick the box but did not make me come out of my new personality – initially crushed and run over, now, however, walled up and stronger than ever. In the old days I would go straight back home. Yet Soho had so many temptations and after all I was still young – in my twenty-ninth year of life – and an attractive Eastern European with sad eyes. No, Tom shouldn't feel uncomfortable, shouldn't feel that I may leave him... Forty-year-old-middle-aged-doctor-with-two-kids... No, he shouldn't suffer...poor Tom...me on my own in Soho, I should not do it to him.

A few minutes later I realized that that was exactly the reason why he had had an affair – I was the good-looking one, who everyone would say must have shagged lots of blokes during these six years... But the fact is... I had not. I have been faithful, waiting at home when Tom was travelling or preparing everything for our time with the kids. He was the one who was the breadwinner and who left everything else on my head. The one who, at the medical school where he held a chair, was promoted twice during the time we were together, while I didn't make any progress on the personal level myself. I turned immediately and went back to Old Compton Street and entered the first café I saw. It was French and behind the till there was an East Asian lady serving, struggling to understand her American customer's requests.

"...no, I don't want a lemon water. I would like a tea with a slice of lemon in it!"

She turned to her friend and said, "Can't they send them for some courses of decent English?" and gave her a sarcastic grin.

The lady behind the till heard and understood every word, which seemed to be the intention of her customer. She responded kindly in her broken English.

"Please find seat, I bring..." giving the old pompous cow a big, honest smile.

I ordered a slice of blueberry tart and a tea and started to look for a quiet seat. The place was packed and some of the tables were shared. I saw the large American woman still standing, looking for a table – she seemed to be waving among the crowd like an old transatlantic ship on a stormy sea. Someone just stood up in the corner – the table was big, with four seats and close to me. I decided that, forgetting about any courtesy and good manners, I would get it so that this wretched woman would have to make her swings and turns for a bit longer.

Shortly after my order arrived, brought by the lovely Asian lady (I instantly decided to like her!). By this stage all my attention was on somebody else, standing by the till. A lady of advanced age and on the short side, was in the company of another, younger, blonde and very pretty girl. The old woman was extremely ugly, with a frog face, all bejewelled with the sort of New-Age-gipsy type of ornaments and with a funky scarf around her neck. There was something fascinating about her and her strongly foreign accent. She sounded like a Russian aristocrat who had lived for many years in Western Europe. My dreamy nature could already imagine her being thrown out of her splendid palace by the crowd of vicious and bloodthirsty red revolutionists. But then my sanity reminded me that to be alive during the Russian Revolution the woman would have to be nearly a hundred today, even though she still would have been only a baby then. My theory didn't meet the reality – she was far too young for that, despite the fact that she might have been in her late seventies. She ordered for herself and for the young girl, a tea and two rhubarb tarts, not allowing her to say a word. While the Asian lady was putting the order through the till, the old woman said quite loud to her companion, "I adore rhubarb tart, it reminds me of the ancient regime..."

My intuition was right! There was a mystery behind her, maybe an exile, and the loss of possessions and a dashing aristocratic lover dying during the war. And now maybe she was living in a little studio flat, here in Soho, having as neighbours a transvestite-turned-night-time-performer, a gay yoga teacher, a stiff collar fund manager and two druggies with a dog. She would get on with them very well, inviting them for afternoon tea served in the Meissen china cups from the old set of her ancestors. She would read them poems translated from Russian and draw their little portraits with charcoal pencils, staining permanently her white bony fingers.

She began to talk again and I was all ears by now, completely ignoring the book I got for myself to read.

"It is so lovely to see you, darling, and you are just like your grandmother used to be…so pretty and full of life…"

The girl only smiled, covering her shyness, being slightly intimidated by how loud the old lady was.

Suddenly, the unthinkable happened: the old woman had struggled to find a seat and without any hesitation, she proceeded to walk in the direction of a big table in the corner, occupied by me. I felt that she had discovered my nosiness… and my desire to give her a hug because she reminded me so much of the many sisters of my granny, relicts of the ancient pre-war prosperity and class. She reminded me of home. And, anyway, who wouldn't like to hug an old woman with an internal class who would hold you with her bejewelled, curved by rheumatism, fingers.

"Excuse me, I have noticed that you are sitting on your own and there is such a crowd here today – would you awfully mind if we joined you? Promise not to interrupt your studies…"

For a second I thought she meant me, studying her character and conversations, and I felt ashamed that I was not a gentleman, that I did listen to every word she was saying before. But then I realized that she meant a book on my table and I felt immediately easier about the entire situation.

"No, not at all," I gave her my best smile, still half embarrassed.

"Pass me that shawl, dear," she said to the young companion.

I quickly turned to my book, pretending that I was reading and that the book was really captivating. As a matter of fact I couldn't get a word of what was in front of me and I caught my sight nervously jumping all around the pages.

"Do you like rhubarb, sweetheart? In our days it was such a popular ingredient of every desert but now somehow it fell out of favour and I have to come here for my tart," she sent a smile to the blonde girl.

"Yes – we have rhubarb in our garden."

"Do you have a garden in Budapest?" the old woman interrupted quite abruptly.

"No..." It was obvious that for the young girl having a proper conversation in English was a struggle; her English was far too formal and very proper – a mistake so common amongst foreigners – "...in Budapest we have an apartment but Grandmother have a little house in the country with a big garden and a fruit trees garden—"

"An orchard, you mean, darling." She interrupted her again.

"Yes, an orchard," she corrected herself and seemed to be quite intimidated by the old woman.

In this very moment a young and hunky man sitting next to us stood up from his table and left. My foreign neighbour looked at me sending me a smile again... It was obvious she wanted me to move to that table. Her look seemed to be pushing me to do it and her facial expression was making me leave the table that was mine. As it often happens with people with a strong will and an ability to manipulate...she got her way, as I did move.

"Are you sure, young man?" she asked me when I rose from my seat.

"Yes, it seems much more comfortable and will allow you some privacy."

"And you will be able to study in silence..." Not only had she managed to take a seat by my table and then made me move, but now it seemed that she was doing me a favour with the entire swap! My fascination with her had increased by now and could only have been explained either by the fact that I was brought up in a very bossy and controlling family or that I must have been the latest victim of the Stockholm syndrome.

"Indeed, it will be much more suitable," I confirmed, despite the fact that I did not even come here to study.

When I sat down in my new place, two rhubarb tarts arrived at my neighbours' table. I started drinking tea and was still listening carefully, with a higher level of impatience. But then a surprise came – the old woman started to talk quietly, more intimately with the girl; it was obvious that her previous behaviour was only for show.

"Those are drugs, my dear..." I could hear and again some idiosyncratic words, "...brother...anger...didn't mean to hit..."

I was boiling in desperation to hear more, but I couldn't. After a few minutes of staring at them I saw something astonishing – a small tear rolled down the face of the young girl...just one pearl-like tear which suddenly made her look not only intimidated but also very vulnerable. The old woman also changed her look – she was now a concerned matron, someone who was guiding her and taking her under her wing. The young woman wasn't eating much, while the old one was digging her fork into a tart with the greed of a person who is not allowed such treats. I noticed that when her piece was finished, she dug into the one belonging to the girl.

The conversation got increasingly quieter now and was only, from time to time, interrupted by the difficult to understand words, which sounded like some foreign names of people or places. Then I saw the old woman giving a nod to the staff, obviously asking for their attention. The Asian woman came over.

"Was the service included in the bill, my dear?"

"Yes, madam."

"You make a fantastic rhubarb tart, jolly good really." She put her hand into a coat pocket and on the small glass tray she placed some noisy coins.

"Thank you, madam—"

"Don't say thank you," she again interrupted, "you deserved it, my dear, every penny of it."

A few minutes later they stood up and started to put their coats on. I felt panic – I didn't know what happened and I wanted to know. More now than ever before.

The old woman turned right from her table and was now heading towards me. Again! She came closer and began to search for something in her big, hippy-like sack-bag. She found it and put it on my table. It was a little chocolate wrapped in a gold, very sophisticated looking foil.

"You are not very happy, young man. But other people's stories will not heal the harm that was done to your heart. You will have to deal with all the pain by yourself and only then you will understand how important it is to be always your own person. And don't worry, all will be fine. It always is in the end…"

And she was gone, leaving me behind…totally mesmerized…

The Thai Adventure

The drinks had just arrived. A slender Thai waiter put a Mojito next to Ghislaine's deckchair and topped up the glass next to Karel with water and ice. The last two days in Phuket had been extremely relaxing, especially after several days spent previously in Bangkok.

Karel looked at Ghislaine but she didn't seem to be present. He followed her sight and, as he suspected, it was focused on the young, exceptionally toned Italian who arrived with his girlfriend only the previous night. The hotel was full of middle-aged, well-to-do people and the only guests below thirty were the Italians and Karel. The place was very slick, reflecting quite correctly the marketing slogan on its website which Karel saw when he booked the: "Modern luxury with a kiss of sun". And, indeed, it was magnificent. Karel felt very happy that, eventually, he had Ghislaine just for himself, without all these hoity-toity people, back in Paris. He felt that there, in Thailand, Ghislaine was only his and that, maybe, she would also start showing him, just like in the old days, some signs of her feelings.

Their relationship had lasted for nearly three years now and Karel knew that it may not be forever. But he hoped. When they met he had fallen in love with her at the very first sight.

She was glamorous and successful but, more importantly, she had a defined personality and Karel found that element of her extremely fascinating. Women of his age were nearly always immature while Ghislaine came across as confident, with an understanding of her expectations and tastes. When Karel met Ghislaine he had been going through a very difficult period, struggling for years with depression. Being very sensitive and shy by nature, he had always had difficulty starting new relationships. Meeting Ghislaine allowed him to experience love and acceptance. It also gave him confidence, helped him to change his outlook on life and to recover. At the very beginning Karel believed that he and Ghislaine could be perfectly happy together. For Ghislaine, nearly fifteen years of age difference was something much less easy to accept. She was worried what her children might say, or her girlfriends. They eventually got together, mostly due to the persistency of Karel. But life hadn't been easy for either of them since, and Karel was wondering if she thought about separation as often as he did. Not because he didn't love her, but, paradoxically, because he loved her so much. He couldn't stand her suffering whenever a younger woman was sending him a smile and he couldn't take anymore of her getting attention from men of her age, with huge success under their belts. Success he could not possibly achieve. Not now, not ever.

The worst part was... Karel's appearance. He was very slim, if not skinny, and with his blonde hair and a fair complexion, Karel looked like he was in his early twenties, if not younger. That led to many funny situations, like the one when he was asked for ID while buying wine, but some were less amusing and so much more hurtful for Ghislaine. Once in Paris when they were dining out in a restaurant with her two kids, the waiter took Karel for another of Ghislaine's children. Tonia and Louis loved the idea, but Ghislaine didn't take it well. She didn't speak to Karel for nearly ten days afterwards, punishing him for something that so obviously wasn't his fault.

"How is your book, honey?" Karel asked Ghislaine, who very quickly took her sight off the perfectly shaped bottom of the handsome Italian and turned towards her read.

"Rather boring and the author is dragging it a bit..." She wasn't very present and Karel didn't know whether it was because of the other guy, the heat or simply that she wasn't in a good mood. He was always worried when she was falling into this state as that meant an argument. Over the years Karel learnt how to handle those situations, though he never felt very comfortable with them. Ghislaine was very moody, which often meant a sudden blow even in the middle of the most perfect evening together. It was always so unexpected and could be triggered by the smallest of events, which others might have not even noticed.

"Are you OK, G?" He always called her by the first letter of her name.

"Why? Is there anything wrong with me?" She took her iPhone out and was checking her reflection in its screen.

"No, you look very pretty today...just thought that something might be wrong..."

"Jesus Christ! I asked you to stop worrying about me. I am good and in the end I am allowed to be in a bad mood, aren't I? I am a grown woman, Karel! I can't take any more of it. I need a drink." She stood up and walked towards the bar.

By then Karel knew that something was definitely happening. Ghislaine was worrying about something or maybe felt guilty about not taking the kids with them. She always behaved in this way when she was displeased and Karel was the one who had to take the hit. He knew that from that moment that not only would the entire day be difficult, but the evening may also not go well. And he planned a surprise dinner for her that night; on the beach, with the candles, just the two of them.

Ghislaine was walking back.

"I cannot find anyone who can bring me a drink. The place looked so good when we arrived but as soon as they got us they stopped caring. I am going back to the room – I am going to stay there all day. I am bored of this fucking place!"

"Ghislaine," Karel grabbed her hand which she immediately pulled back, "please, whatever it is, you know we can talk about it. I am here and I love you. We are in this amazing place... Just on our own, together..."

"I would much rather be at home now. I am tired of this place and I am tired of you. You simply annoyed me and ruined my day. Can't you just have your own life? I feel with you like I am stuck. Grow some balls, Karel." Ghislaine walked off again.

Karel knew that there was nothing he could have done. He also knew that it wasn't his fault. Whatever was bothering her was in her mind. Ghislaine was a self-made woman – from a very modest background, where there was no money and plenty of alcohol problems. Her parents were so focused on themselves and their drinking that they didn't even try to establish any relationship with Ghislaine's children, who saw their grandparents only once a year for Christmas. As a result, Tonia and Louis treated them like strangers and often confused their names.

Karel could see that, as much as Ghislaine's parents

loved her, they were never able to show her deeper feelings as they simply didn't have any. He understood how difficult it must have been for Ghislaine to be amongst other people, from a completely different background, and to fit in. She was a wealthy and successful woman of the world, but she went abroad for the first time when she was twenty-five, using the savings from her first job. She gained a place at an elite private university before that and was working every weekend to pay the fees and to keep herself going. Having no time for friends or even a boyfriend, she grew isolated, distant to others and with a lack of social skills. Now, many years later, Ghislaine was a very popular host of many parties, thrown in one of her two spacious houses, and she had in her contact list the phone numbers of nearly everyone in the latest edition of *Who's Who*. But Karel knew it was all a game. The persistent fight to gain recognition and acceptance from others had cost her a lot and there were not many situations when she was her real self anymore. Karel loved her the way she was, under the make-up of social conventions. Being a good judge of character, he could see all her decent nature and he was able to acknowledge the reasons for her strange behaviour. He also had no doubts that one day she would find peace and would stop struggling so much. And he was hoping to be there and to enjoy this moment with her.

"Hello, old sport! How are you doing today?"

Karel lifted his hand to cover the sun and to be able to see the newcomer. He must have fallen asleep and now he felt angry that he'd lost so much of the day. The sun, in the shape of a red orange, was already coming down to the ocean.

As he suspected, it was Daniel. Good old Daniel. Many years ago he had worked with Ghislaine in Brussels until he decided that the world of finance was not his cup of tea and he moved to Thailand in order to pursue a new career path… He was now a yoga teacher.

"Hey… Dan…great to see you." The truth was – it wasn't.

Daniel was a very honest and open person but since they invited him for dinner a few days ago he had come to the hotel every day. So they had to buy him lunch or dinner or both and to spend time with him before they managed to find an excuse to go off and do their own thing. One day, when Ghislaine had been in a good mood, they just ran away together along the beach to the neighbouring hotel, in order to avoid him. This trip was about them being together, not about hosting and socializing.

"Where is Ghislaine?"

"She just went to the villa to get something to drink. You know what? Let's go and surprise her," Karel suggested and thought that using Daniel was a great excuse to destroy a wall which Ghislaine always built around herself in situations like this one. He knew that she would have to be civil in front of Daniel.

"Are you sure? Am I not intruding?" asked Daniel.

"Nonsense, don't be ridiculous. She would love to see you."

When they got to the villa Ghislaine was on a daybed in the ocean view sitting room.

"Are you resting, honey?" Karel quickly asked and before Ghislaine managed to respond abruptly he added quite loudly, "Daniel is here and would like to see you, darling."

Ghislaine jumped from the bed and instantly wrapped herself with a long silk tunic-dress in a flower design.

"Where is he?" she whispered. "Oh, how fantastic!" she said aloud.

"In the corridor," Karel responded.

She gave him an angry look with her lips characteristically clenched.

"Daniel! It is great to see you! How are you? Do get in and fix yourself a drink, darling..."

Now they were all three of them in the small sitting room of the villa. They could hear waves breaking onto the beach. The ocean was very stormy that day.

"How are you doing, chaps?" Daniel asked with his artificially styled Oxford accent.

"We are very well. Really. Aren't we, darling?" Ghislaine desperately looked towards Karel.

"Yes, we have had a marvellous day." Karel came to the rescue and smiled at her. She smiled back. Her tensed face muscles seemed to let go and she looked much more relaxed and pleasant. "We were sunbathing and swimming in the ocean and Ghislaine nearly finished reading her book."

"What was that?" Daniel asked looking at Ghislaine.

"Sorry?" she asked back and her face tensed again.

"The book, you silly sausage..."

"Ah," she was relaxed again, "*Paradise Forgotten* by Terence Brown."

"I read it! Incredible book, so captivating, don't you think?" Daniel was in an intellectual mood today.

"Yes, I was just saying to Karel what a fantastic book it was. So real and powerful, really..." She looked at Karel and they exchanged a smile.

"What plans do you have for tonight?" Daniel asked.

"We are invited to dinner by the people next door," Karel quickly answered.

Ghislaine looked surprised but didn't say a thing.

"Yes, we refused them twice and, although we would much rather stay in tonight, we have to go, really." Ghislaine thought that adding 'really' at the end of every sentence was making her more sophisticated and she enjoyed the idea that no one knew where she originally came from.

"Is it that late?" Ghislaine looked at the clock above the fireplace. "Karel, we have to start getting ready."

"In that case I will leave you in peace." Daniel stood up from his seat.

"Are you sure you wouldn't like to stay for one more drink at least?" Karel tried to be polite, thinking that Ghislaine was a bit too obvious in her statement, only to realize that Daniel, not being very bright, didn't notice a thing and his response was a simple reaction dictated by good manners.

"You need to get ready, guys. I hate rushing when I am going out," Daniel confirmed. Karel felt sorry for Daniel – it was obvious to everybody that Daniel was very lonely in Thailand. Due to the lack of potential people who could keep him company or for any other reasons, he knew hardly anyone and was coming across as very sad and painfully on his own.

"Do come to see us again, darling," Ghislaine added, "It would be jolly good to see you before we leave in two days, really…"

"I will see what I can do. I'll let you know anyway." Daniel kissed Ghislaine on her cheek, shook hands with Karel and left.

"Now I really need a drink," Ghislaine said and she laughed. They hugged and Ghislaine took Karel's hand and kissed it.

"You will never leave me, handsome, will you?"

"Of course I won't. You are my other half and one can have only one other half."

They kissed again.

When Ghislaine went into the bathroom to take a shower, Karel called the beachfront restaurant and booked a table for two. He thought that a dinner on the beach which he had planned for today was a bit premature, considering that they only just managed to soften the tensions caused by the latest argument.

An hour later they were both heading to the restaurant. Ghislaine was wearing the latest dress from Diane von Furstenberg, which highlighted her perfect waistline. Karel, in his white linen shirt and bright-blue cotton trousers with rolled-up legs, looked like one of the Riviera playboys and he felt very confident.

As soon as they entered the restaurant he noticed that people sitting at several tables occupied every night by the Russians looked at them and quite visibly smiled to each other. He had seen it everywhere here. The rich Russians he often met in the south of France were very confident but also perfectly well mannered and discrete. The ones he could see in Thailand were rather vulgar and all fit the same description: an old, visibly obese man, with a younger, dyed-blonde woman. Those women didn't look like the attractive models he saw in the Cote-d'Azure who accompanied rich Russian investors whilst in France. Here they were middle-aged, or at least looked middle-aged, and many of them were only slightly less vulgar than common prostitutes. And now they, of all people, seemed to be amused by a younger man holding the hand of a middle-aged woman.

The day before Karel had seen a group of Russians also laughing at the two Spanish gay guys staying in the next-door villa, very much in love with each other. He also noticed them joking at a mixed-race couple from Canada. Karel knew how rude, thick and intolerant some Russians abroad could be. He was just hoping that now he would not have to experience this with Ghislaine. For him it would mean nothing, for her, however, it could be a truly traumatic experience. He looked at her. She was pale and was trying to put on a show. Karel knew she noticed them too.

They sat down and very quickly placed an order. They didn't speak much. Ghislaine was looking towards the ocean.

"I am so happy to be here with you, Ghislaine..." Karel started.

She didn't look at him, just smiled very nervously.

"Honey, I know what you think... Please stop it. We have each other and it really doesn't matter what other people think about it. About us..."

"It does to me," she turned her head to him and in her eyes there were tears. "I have enough of people looking at me and thinking that I am an old woman and that you do me a favour..."

"But, Ghislaine, you know I love you for who you are... Because and despite of everything... You are the most amazing woman I have ever met in my life and I really think one cannot have more..."

"For me this is not enough," she raised her voice, "Who do you think you are? Some boy who doesn't even have a proper job? I have to pay your bills like you're my toyboy! You are a loser! Did you hear me? Total loser! Worthless!"

Karel looked around. Everyone was staring. One of

the Russian women was giggling without any attempt to hide it. He stood up and, walking at his usual pace, left the restaurant. Karel was pale and his blue veins stood out on his white hands.

Ghislaine left the table soon after him and went to the beach. She was walking, holding her shoes in her hands, stepping with determination into the sand. In the ocean, up to their knees, there were some people fishing crabs. She felt angry with herself. Couldn't Karel see that she was madly in love with him? Couldn't he understand that all this was her insecurity and mess inside of her head? She knew she must find some help. Otherwise she would destroy herself, but more importantly would destroy Karel...and the children.

She looked around and took a deep breath. Suddenly she felt right and could see clearly. Yes, she was going to find some help! She would sort it out! There were psychologists out there. And she could afford a good one. The best in his class. She was now light and easy and couldn't understand why she was so angry and frustrated before. She had to go to Karel and apologize. And tomorrow they would come down for a breakfast and would smile into the faces of those Russian assholes.

She ran to the villa. When she entered, it was dark.

"Honey! I am back...where are you? I want to apologize. I am sometimes such a bitch. Please forgive me."

She was still walking in the darkness trying to find a light switch. She turned the lights on eventually. And Karel was there. In the middle of the room. Hanging. By his belt. He'd left the terrace door open and now the ocean breeze was moving his slim hanging body.

Ghislaine didn't say a word. She stood for a while. Then

she walked towards the body. Towards Karel. She touched his hand and pressed it against her cheek. He will wake up and in the morning she will tell him how much she loves him...

A Date

I stood in the hallway with a feeling of total inadequacy – the one we experience when we are about to try something new and different. Something that scares us but something we know we have to do.

I looked around the apartment. It was, by far, the best part of the day in my new little place. The sun was striking the only window of my sitting room. The flat was on the lower ground floor and had only one bedroom but I had just bought it and felt very proud that I possessed my own 'little pad' in London. The apartment wasn't big but was spacious enough to fit all my books and a vast collection of my pre-war family photos. I had spent the entire previous night unpacking and putting all the things in their place. Despite the fact that it was only my second night here I wanted to feel at home as soon as possible. And now I had to leave this cosy arrangement in order to step onto a path of the unknown. I had to, yet again, go out and meet a man I had never met before. I had to tell him something funny and something catchy and strike a perfect balance between being intelligent but not too heavy and overwhelming, amusing but not too shallow. God, how I hated the idea of dating. And for the past seven years I thought that these sorts of experiences would never happen to me again. And I did not miss it. I liked the stability and security of my life, but Simon decided to change it. And today I wasn't looking forward to going for my first, in nearly eight years, date. I loathed the idea of it.

I locked the front door and walked one floor up, to the main lobby. A tall man was entering the building. I knew he was a retired colonel in the army and that he was divorced too. The manager of the building, Jenny, briefed me on many details of the residents when I came to view the flat several months ago. She took my email address under the pretext that she could answer many of my queries regarding the building and since then she was bombarding my mail box with all the information about the private lives of my neighbours with a disturbing regularity. She clearly had not much going on in her own life or maybe she was just very proud that she possessed so many of the secrets of Chelsea's upper classes. As a result I knew of my neighbours who'd got divorced, I knew who was estranged from their children and...who also was gay, apart from myself, obviously.

I said hello to the Colonel and he politely responded, clearly not knowing who I was. When I left the building I realized that despite the sun shining, it was also raining at the same time which I could not see from my 'level' of the building. I stood under the porch and searched in my rucksack for an umbrella, which I have always carried with me. After all, in London one has to be prepared for sudden changes of weather. I looked ahead at Burton's Court and then left towards the Royal Chelsea Hospital and I felt proud again. I hereby possessed my own part of Chelsea, maybe tiny, but in a prime spot. The sense of achievement, for a brief second, took the pressure off my upcoming date. I was comfortable with myself and my life and didn't see any reasons why I could not go out for a date with anyone. I was thirty-five and as a result of going to the gym regularly, I looked better than ever. I was educated and I had my own apartment in Chelsea. I could have anybody and Simon could fuck himself.

I turned towards the Saatchi Gallery and decided to take a cab to the Victoria & Albert Museum. It wasn't far away from where I was and I could have walked but I didn't want Mark to see me tired or sweaty or looking in any other way than I would like to appear at my date. We passed by Sloane Square and then down Sloane Street, at the end of which we turned left onto Brompton Road. The museum was on my right hand side and as we came closer to it, I felt increasing panic. Maybe it wasn't such a good idea. Maybe I shouldn't have started dating. Maybe it was too early. My decree absolute arrived only last week and here I was going for a date. It definitely was too early and I should go back home. I should have a bath or just watch *Gone with the Wind* and stay indoors. I wasn't ready for it yet. As I was about to ask the driver to turn back and take me home, I thought about Simon. I thought how smug he was with his new boyfriend, with their new houseboat in Putney. He was not going to have the satisfaction of seeing me defeated. No, I was going to get out of this cab and have the best afternoon ever.

When I met Simon I was twenty-eight. He was a couple of years older and swept me off my feet. I know it is old-fashioned to think in this way and not many people do anymore but I really hoped that my quest for happiness had ended. I was sure that we were meant to be together. But things hardly ever go the way we plan them. So after seven years together, four of which were in a civil partnership, it came as a surprise that Simon decided to change the entire arrangement. The only problem was that he decided to change it for himself, forgetting that this meant an unavoidable transformation for me too. He was leaving me for a twenty-four-year-old, skinny, Argentinian dancer – Jorge. I saw them together and they looked 'divine' or at least this is one of those words that Jorge would use to describe them. And now they had a houseboat, which was Simon's and my dream for the past three years and in three months they will have a child. A child which Simon promised me we would have, though he postponed this decision every year, using different arguments. "Let's wait for a while until things settle," he used to say whenever I asked for a date we could start searching for a surrogate mother. He never defined 'a while' and now I think I should have requested from him to specify this term. I should have done that before I felt so certain about my future and about our future, together. The separation went easily – we split what we had and neither of us really fought for more. We both seemed to understand the significance of the dissolution of our partnership, though to a different extent. For me it was the end of a chapter I wasn't ready to end, for him it was the end of the chapter before entering into a new chapter, which he had already started to write. At least we both agreed that there was a chapter. I didn't feel angry anymore but only sad and hurt. Like a person who buries a part of himself forever, at the same time burying his best friend too, because I have always considered Simon to be my best friend.

Now I knew I had to meet Mark. The past had to be cut off, no matter how painful it was to be. I paid for the taxi and walked into the museum.

The Victoria and Albert Museum was always one of those places where I felt comfortable regardless of what was happening to me and what frame of mind I was in. I have always thought that this was one of the most exciting museums, not because it presented a dazzling collection of art but because it was so diverse, spacious and visionary. Entering there was like having an insight into the brain of a genius artist: unpredictable, surprising, horizon-broadening. When during our online correspondence Mark asked me where I would like to meet, I picked the V&A without hesitation. I also chose it because I knew that Simon hated it and I was determined to show Mark how much it meant to me. This time I wanted to start my new relationship, no matter how long-lasting, on the basis of being honest with who I was and what I was standing by.

Mark and I 'met' online. Several years ago everyone was afraid to admit it and people would always make up some stories how they bumped into each other in a café or in a nightclub. But, I discovered soon after I went back to the dating market, now it had become trendy. It somehow fitted into our new exhibitionistic human nature, in a world where everyone seems to find it crucial to share with the entire population what they ate, who they slept with and what is their 'relationship status'. I have always had a strong belief that Facebook, Twitter or Instagram are nothing other than a shop window in which we can shamelessly show ourselves to others, regardless of whether there is anyone who is actually interested or not. Just like in the Red Light District in Amsterdam where prostitutes push themselves into the arms of the uninterested tourists. Having nothing to offer, desperate to get noticed and sell.

Mark emailed me first and I emailed back. We seemed to be very different but somehow the correspondence went smoothly and we were writing to each other more every day. It had been nearly three weeks since we had started and Mark suggested that we should meet. He made no illusions about the purpose of this meeting: "to check whether we are wasting each other's time". This sounded like turning a date into an exam. And although Mark knew everything about my relationship history, he didn't know exactly how I felt about my past and about dates in general. How uncomfortable I felt with the entire dating culture, I should have said. But I have learnt that it is healthy not to say everything we think, and I decided to keep my fears to myself. Insecurity can be off-putting and I didn't want to lose a chance to see Mark, because he was really good-looking and seemed to be intelligent and funny, and also because we really were getting on, if it is possible to make this sort of assumption without meeting someone in the flesh.

We were supposed to meet in my favourite place – in the Cast Court, by the copy of the Trajan's Column. I was walking fast, being quite impatient by nature. I decided that if I was going to meet him, it was better to have the difficulties of the first handshake behind us. But when I got there, there was nobody there. I mean, obviously, apart from dozens of tourists from around the world. He must have changed his mind, I thought. Why wouldn't he? Who am I to have a good-looking and clever boyfriend? I should have stayed at home... And then I saw him. He was entirely drenched by the rain. The water was dripping off his ears and he was walking quickly like he didn't want to be late. He noticed me and smiled.

"You must be Adam," Mark said. "I was soooooo looking forward to meeting you," and he kissed me on the cheek, although I didn't even manage to stretch my hand for a handshake.

"Hi, Mark, it is good to see you in the flesh." What was I saying? It sounded ridiculous. Now he definitely wouldn't want to go out with me. I sounded like a middle-aged, boring prig who would rather play croquet than be going for dates…

"I am sorry I am late. I came by bike and I could not find a place to park it. I am ashamed to admit it – although I am a Londoner – I have never been here before. But then I have lived here only for thirty-eight years," and he smiled with ease, naturally.

"It is never too late for anything." No, I sounded like my granddad. I was stiff and this was definitely going to be our last meeting.

"Where shall we go?" Mark asked.

"Shall we just wander around?" I responded in desperation. I really wanted him to stay and I wanted to be on this date because Mark looked much better than the pictures he had sent me.

He was at least six foot two (I have always had a thing for tall men), with broad shoulders and a swimmer's build. He had a Samurai haircut – very short hair on the sides with a much longer part left in the middle of his head, which, in turn, was tied into a combination of a ponytail and a bun. He was clean shaven, wearing a fitted white sweatshirt and khaki trousers which were tied to his ankles with special straps. He must have put them on when he was cycling but hadn't removed them since. Mark also had several colourful hand-bands on both his wrists and a stud earring in his left ear. He looked artistic and his New-York-look went very well with his way of speaking. Mark was coming across as confident, experienced and easy to talk to. Everything I was not.

We walked for at least half an hour, not saying much to each other. Or rather Mark was asking questions and I was trying to explain things to him – like I was a tour guide and he was a visitor. He liked Turner's *Venice* and was impressed by the miniatures. He was also very inquisitive about the sculptures, especially the copy of *David* by Michelangelo. I felt that I was failing to impress him, that my answers and comments were not meeting his standards and that he genuinely was bored. But then something else happened.

When we were in the tapestry room, completely on our own and quite overwhelmed by the strong smell of the fabric preservatives, Mark touched me. But it wasn't just a pat or an accidental touch. He came from behind and touched with his index finger the palm of my hand. I had both my hands behind me supporting my back and this gentle, flirtatious move surprised me. I turned back and Mark smiled at me. I smiled back, not knowing really what I was supposed to do. Then Mark just passed me by and walked away towards the tapestry on the opposite side of the room. The situation was repeated several times afterwards, in different rooms. And each time his fingers would touch my hand or my back and gently stroke it. It was just like he was drawing some little emblems there, maybe letters. Suddenly, I realized that Mark might have been writing letters which meant to create words and those were supposed to form a sentence. I felt panic – I did not read them, I did not think. Now, when I did not understand what he tried to tell me, I was definitely going to lose him. He would simply think that I was an idiot and would leave…and I will never see him again… I thought that the only way to end my misery and to limit the paranoia was to go somewhere where we could talk. There I will definitely know what he thinks and where we are at.

"It is really stuffy here today – fancy a coffee?" I asked with hope.

Mark turned back from the cabinet he was just looking at and walked towards me. He took his right hand from his trouser pocket and put it on my right cheek. His hand was warm, big and very masculine. On the top of it there were distinctive veins, which are typical for people who exercise frequently. He looked into my eyes and kissed me. It was a gentle and innocent kiss, after which we both smiled at each other.

"I would love to have a cup of tea," he said.

"Sorry?" I asked, completely forgetting about the question I posed only a few seconds ago.

"You asked me a question about coffee…" he responded.

We both laughed, understanding what had just happened.

In the café, as always, there was a crowd. People were queuing at various stations displaying hot food, cold food, cakes, hot drinks and then queuing again to pay for whatever they picked from all the above. I ordered a coffee while Mark asked for a tea. He also suggested some cakes, remembering clearly our correspondence in which I confessed my admiration for all sorts of bakes.

After paying for our trays we began the usual search for a table both noticing a small table for two alongside the curved wall of the café. The place has always been one of my favourite destinations. I liked the walls with 'over-the-top' tiles, the very modern crystal chandeliers which contrasted sharply with the secessionist decorations and the simple, if not too ordinary, 1950s chairs. It was all in perfect harmony, despite the fact that it did not match, neither in style nor period. In the middle of the room there was also a grand piano. The moment we sat at our table someone took their seat by it.

I looked at Mark and then at our trays. I thought that ordering a scone was a huge mistake on my side, which I realized even more when I noticed his flapjack. He was so handsome and fit and I should not have any more calories than was necessary. Otherwise I would suffocate myself to death trying to breathe in, in order to look slim. It was a habit I'd had since my childhood, but with Mark I realized that I was doing it all the time. And I was already slim, counting daily my calories and following, like a slave, my exercise routines. How many more obsessions could I have? I asked myself and felt amused by my auto-criticism.

Mark was sitting opposite me, admiring the walls and watching other people. Then when the pianist began to play he looked at me. And again he stretched his hand in order to touch mine. I didn't pull it back but left it where it was and I allowed him to hold it.

"'Chan Chan' by Buena Vista Social Club. I love this song!" I said spontaneously.

"I so love Cuban music. I think he also does a great job by twisting it into such a jazzy piece," Mark seemed to be at home with this subject.

"I would never have thought we liked the same music. You have never mentioned anything about it in your emails..." For the first time I felt natural, not embarrassed or intimidated. Just myself, sitting opposite a man who I liked and who I felt equal to.

"My music taste is very broad. I also play the guitar, so I am often trying to play covers of various famous pieces."

"Do you have *any* faults?" I asked and we were both laughing again.

There was a pause in the conversation and we both looked towards the pianist. It was a perfect moment. The mutual understanding we seemed to have, the unique interior of the café and the music from the piano were all complementing each other, creating a truly magical atmosphere. I looked at Mark – he was tanned, well built and had a sparkle in his eyes. I realized how attractive I found him and how much I would like to see him again. And this thought scared me. I was clearly becoming infatuated with someone I didn't know very well, still being deeply hurt by the collapse of my relationship with Simon. I didn't want to be at anybody's mercy again but then the feeling of being adored and to adore was so charming. And I had forgotten how beautiful and fulfilling this could be. It was like being in a fairy tale.

Suddenly the music stopped. The pianist stood up and walked off and into the room entered a new person. A tall, bald man – with facial hair deliberately trimmed so that it looked like he hadn't shaved for a few days – was circling the room in search of a table. He was dark, maybe mixed race, and his navy dotted shirt from Gap was half unbuttoned, showing two large pecs covered with dark chest hair. The man sat by the table next to ours, placing in front of himself a tray with juice and a sandwich.

I looked at Mark but he wasn't looking at me anymore. He was staring at the newcomer, just like most of the gay men and women in the café. I felt like the happy bubble in which I had begun to feel comfortable had burst without any warning. It made me feel angry and frustrated. Mark noticed my impatience. He turned towards me and asked,

"So how do you like to do it?"

"Sorry?" I did not want to believe what I heard.

"I mean, did you like others to join you and your partner? Do you believe in an open relationship?"

I wasn't a prude and have always had various sexual fantasies which I did not mind exploring when I was a single man. But in my relationships I looked for someone who I could be with through thick and thin and to whom I would be faithful to. I also expected this to be reciprocated by my partner. Maybe that was my mistake, maybe gay people were not ready for this progressive, yet old-fashioned at the same time, type of a relationship. Maybe monogamous relationships still did not exist in the vocabulary of many gay men. However, I wanted to entrust my future only to those who could embark with me on this challenge.

"No, I believe in monogamy," I said with some sharpness, surprising even myself with the severity of the statement.

"So you have never thought how cool it would be to be in bed with more than one person?" Mark sounded experienced and knowledgeable on the subject, which only increased my frustration.

"I didn't say I have never done that or wouldn't do it if I was single. I only said that when I am in a relationship, I think it should be monogamous. There are only very few relationships which can survive opening and even those are prone to tensions and jealousy, and they make both parties miserable most of the time. It can be very tempting to be in a relationship and to sleep with many other people at the same time, without expecting any consequences, but they do come. The older we get, the more insecure we feel about it. But then, after years of such understood freedom, it is too late to divert a relationship from that path. Eventually our partner meets someone who only initially is happy with being his occasional adventure and this someone manages to tempt your partner sufficiently to be with him for good and to leave behind all that was built...and to break all the promises that were made. Our partner goes and creates a monogamous relationship with this new person, giving to him everything we could never even ask for. I think that it is not easy to be loyal and faithful but everything that has some sort of value, also has its price. And the more precious our relationship is to us, the higher the price is. But the rewards come too. It is a mutual understanding, respect and security. On this sort of foundation anything can be built."

Mark was set back by the seriousness of my monologue. I was surprised too and felt exhausted. I shared my thoughts and beliefs with someone who obviously wasn't worth it and I started to gather all my things in order to leave.

"Wait!" Mark said. "Please!"

There was a pause and I sat down.

"Listen," Mark started, "I didn't mean any of what I said. I don't even know why I would ask such a ridiculous question. I have never slept with more than one person at the same time and I would never like to. I also believe that we all should try to find someone to live our lives with and that everyone has 'the other half' somewhere out there. Only one 'other half'... I am so sorry. I am very shy and I hate dating and I never know what to say or do on dates. It is just so difficult to pretend this confidence while one would just like to be with someone else. To feel the warmth and to be attracted to someone. To listen and to be listened to. The truth is that I like you. As a matter of fact, I like you very much. And you are way out of my league with all your degrees and your looks. I know this, but I just would like you to give me a chance..."

"When I met you, I thought you were out of my league too. All this sporty lifestyle and fashionable looks... I couldn't possibly keep up with this..." We both smiled.

"So will you see me again?" Mark asked.

I wasn't sure what to say. I didn't know whether, considering my out-of-proportion outburst, I was ready to date again. I liked Mark but, over the years, I'd been hurt too much and I felt I needed some peace and space.

"Let's see..." I answered.

Mark looked seriously upset but he made a final attempt:

"I could take you to Ronnie Scott's next Saturday...we could go as friends. There is no pressure and we could just take it from there. Please, just one more date and you will make up your mind then..."

"OK. Ronnie Scott's...as friends..." I smiled.

He looked relieved and I felt flattered. No one had fought to have a date with me with a similar persistency for a very long time.

We said goodbye to each other in front of the building, kissing each other on the cheek.

I walked towards Knightsbridge with the hope of catching a taxi somewhere around Harrods. It had started to rain again and I realized that I didn't have my umbrella with me. I must have left it in the café. I hesitated whether to go back. It was warm and I felt good. For the first time in many months I felt free and confident and it was all thanks to Mark. I decided not to go back for the umbrella and to walk home. The way I was. In the rain. I soon felt drenched as the rain strengthened but it was like being born again. Everything seemed to be intense, but it was a good intense. I felt at peace with myself. And I decided that the next day I would text Mark. Maybe we could go for a coffee or a drink during the week. Next Saturday seemed to be ages away...

The English Divorce

Sam got into the car. She hit the wheel with her open hands several times.

"Son of a bitch! Son of a bitch!" she was screaming. Tears were dropping from her eyes onto the horn and from there to a floor of the car. "I am going to kill him! I will send him to the cleaners! Bastard! Fucking bastard!" she was talking to herself.

Sam and Ralph, her husband of eight years, were living in a fashionable West-London neighbourhood. Their seven-bedroom house could be, by many, called 'aspirational'. Growing up in a scruffy flat, in the nearby council estate, made Sam acknowledge at a very early stage of her life what sort of home was her dream, and her current address made her proud of what she and Ralph had achieved. At the house Sam would always take every guest on a tour of the rooms, even if such a trip was not requested. She would show them all four reception rooms and the swimming pool and the gym with the sauna, situated in the basement, especially dug out for that purpose.

The entire house, from flooring to the door handles, was designed by well-known interior designers and compensating for everything that was missing in Sam's past.

Or at least what she felt that was missing.

Sam grew up in a household of her single mother and much older brother and their only income was from state benefits. She knew from the very beginning that she had to find a way to get out of the poverty and the lack of prospects which overshadowed her mother's life. Sam wasn't academic. She struggled at school but had gone to middling university and managed to secure an unremarkable degree in religious education. Without the prestige of a top university behind her and with no career prospects based on family connections, the only way to climb out of poverty seemed to be to marry someone whose life wouldn't have all these hurdles. Someone who could give her everything she never had and who would help her to run away from her past.

She was already well into her thirties when she met Ralph. It happened at Pamela's birthday party. Pamela was Sam's friend, or at least that is how Sam referred to her. In fact, Pamela was a much more senior work colleague, from a very well-to-do family. From the moment when Sam started to work as a research assistant in the head offices of a large charity organization, she immediately noticed Pamela. And from that day Sam did everything that was in her power to befriend her, or at least to get into her world as deeply as possible. Sam changed her clothes and her haircut. She ceased to paint her nails a strong red colour, swapping it for a white-pearl, the same one Pamela used. She wore long, flowery scarves and had started to speak using very few, consciously chosen words, with a much more sophisticated accent.

After several months of attempts Sam eventually managed to get noticed by Pamela and occasionally both women would go for lunch together. Sometimes Pamela would also invite Sam to social gatherings in her apartment in Bayswater, which overlooked Kensington Gardens and Hyde Park. Spread over the entire floor of the building, it was tastefully furnished with big pieces of modern art and industrial re-adapted furniture. Instantly it became a dream home for Sam. A home which she would like to have herself, one day.

On the night of the birthday party Pamela's apartment seemed to be bursting with people. In fact, more people came than the four-bedroom two-reception room flat could take and groups of people were not only standing in the kitchen and on the two balconies but also in the hallway and the main bathroom. The music was discreet and many lamps were replaced for the night by candle lampions positioned in the corners of the rooms. Waiters with the trays of smoked-salmon canapés had to squeeze into the crowd, holding the food high up above people's heads, apologizing each time they did this manoeuvre.

Sam had drunk a few glasses of wine already and was on her way to the toilet when she saw Ralph. He was a few years older than her and was engaged in a conversation with another man. Ralph was wearing a smart suit, just like most of the men at the party who had come straight from work, but he looked different to many of the other men. He seemed to be very comfortable with himself and very smart. At the same time he was coming across as very shy. Sam was never shy and even at her primary school she had been willing to argue with her teachers in order to defend her opinions. However, on that day, in Pamela's apartment, all the qualities and characteristics of Ralph were of minor importance. There was one thing about Ralph which Sam liked from the very beginning and this element was overshadowing everything else she thought of him. Ralph was visibly very well off and back then, on that night, Sam's instinct was telling her she was going to marry him one day.

Since then Sam and Ralph, who indeed married seven months after the party at Pamela's, had had two sons, Jean-Pierre and Gianfranco. The names of the boys were French and Italian, although neither Sam nor Ralph had any French or Italian ancestors. Sam chose them because they sounded unusual and, in connection with Ralph's English surname hinted at the comfortable background of their parents. Sam believed that those names would automatically place her children way above the social standing she could have ever had with hers and she was very conscious to make such a statement.

After moving homes several times, Sam and Ralph eventually acquired Waterheights, a spacious red-brick mansion in which they lived until that day. The house was refurbished at great cost and, while Ralph was at work and the children were at school, Sam had it just for herself.

Sam stopped working the day after she came back from the African honeymoon with Ralph. They did not need the money. Ralph, who was an architect, had his own practice, which he had inherited from his father, with the well-established company's name, and a portfolio of assets. This wealth took all the pressure off him to keep a job though he chose to work. He loved his job, despite the long hours and stress connected to running his own practice, and he felt very proud of his designs.

"I have to talk to you, Sam," Ralph entered their double-height sitting room.

Sam was just placing flowers in a vase. She enjoyed doing it and roses were her favourite.

"What is it, Ralph? Just talk to me now – I can do two things at the same time," and she smiled towards him. It wasn't an honest smile though. The truth was that their marriage began to deteriorate rapidly after the first six months, and the disagreements grew over the following years. Constant arguments and tensions could not be explained only by the fact that Ralph, after all day at work, was often tired. Nor by the fact that after spending the entire day at home Sam sometimes felt frustrated. They just were not getting along and, for quite a while now, they had been heading towards a brick wall with their relationship. But whenever the problems appeared Sam tried to heal them by getting pregnant.

They had indeed tried very hard to have their first child but with the second one, it was Sam who wanted it. Later she just told Ralph that it was an accident.

Neither Sam nor Ralph really liked children. For him, becoming a father was about proving to the world, and to himself, his masculinity. To breed was, in his social class, something that was considered a part of success, just like a good job or a nice house. For Sam having children was about keeping Ralph.

She had understood quickly the very simple principles of the English upper classes and she had mastered them. Their house was always immaculate and the New England style clothes she was wearing or the magazines she read reflected the very basic principles of the stiff upper lip cast.

"I really have to talk to you. Now...please!" Ralph repeated with greater emphasis.

Not again, she thought. For the past several years most

of their evenings ended with an argument. It did not help that they were both drinking heavily every night. Wandering around the house with a big glass filled with red wine for the entire evening was something broadly accepted in this world and days often ended with the slamming door and with them sleeping in different bedrooms. Sam was worried that now Ralph may want to revisit the things they had said to each other, or rather shouted out to each other, the previous night.

They both went into the library and Ralph, who entered after Sam, closed the double door behind them. Sam sat on one of the two parallel sofas positioned in front of the fireplace.

We need another woollen throw here, she thought. The check one I saw in the last *Country Life* would be perfect. Or shall we just buy a third sofa to bring some asymmetry to the room? The idea of redecorating the entire room put her, immediately, in a perfect mood.

"Sam, I am sorry for saying this in this way...actually for saying this at all... I know it sounds rather cruel and you may think I am ruthless but this is the only way I can say it...the only way I can do it... I would like to ask you for a divorce..."

Sam couldn't believe what she had just heard. They were supposed to be together until the end of their lives. They were supposed to look after each other and care for each other and enjoy life when the kids eventually went away to build their own lives. Or at least something along those lines...

Sam had known she didn't love Ralph for a long time by now, if ever. When she met him, he was the answer to her ambitions and insecurities. She convinced herself into marrying him, though there were moments during their relationship when she felt good and comfortable in his company. More often, however, she felt intimidated by his intelligence and his sarcastic sense of humour. She could never understand his jokes and always felt like he was laughing at her. Sam didn't enjoy any of Ralph's hobbies either – she couldn't stand the opera and the thought of visiting stately homes' gardens when they went on holiday gave her a proper chill. The truth was that although Ralph was very good looking, she did not find him attractive and didn't enjoy their sporadic intimate time in the bedroom. But Ralph was a guarantor of her status and sense of belonging and she didn't have any intentions to ever change it. The idea of divorce, not alien to her, was something Sam would never contemplate in these circumstances. She also wasn't going to allow Ralph to contemplate it either.

"Honey, what are you talking about? Did you have a bad day or something? You know very well, just as well as I do, that we passed our peak already but we have two children and we have responsibilities towards them. We are a family and families do not break, even if…"

Sam carried on as she always did. She was always talking without any breaks. She never noticed that the other party wasn't listening. And Ralph was used to it, so he looked back towards the fireplace where, on the mantelpiece, there was a line of framed pictures of their smiling children. There were also pictures of him and Sam on some exotic holiday. All dressed in expensive white clothes, Sam's favourite colour, lying on some hammock. Ralph had no recollections of this trip and he genuinely could not remember a single thing from this holiday, or from so many others. He knew that he had spent all these years with a person he didn't like, even if he had loved her for a brief period.

Ralph was standing there and he felt guilty. He understood that he was taking away something from Sam. Not that their divorce was going to cause her any significant financial detriment. He was going to give her a part of his assets and to house her comfortably. However, she definitely would lose Waterheights and the cosiness of the entire arrangement.

"…so I think that we simply have to calm down and talk about it tomorrow morning when we will be fresher and have had some head space." Sam was very good at convincing people to do things they never wanted to do.

"Sam, you have to understand that I have thought about this for a very long time. We cannot live like this any longer. It is not good for us and not good for the children."

"What are you talking about? The kids are perfectly happy running around in the garden, jumping in the bouncy castle or playing around the house with their many friends. What is not good for them here? Comfort? Or their public schools? What is the matter with you today?"

"Yes, they do have a good life but they are living with parents who do not love each other, who are not happy…"

"Who is not happy here? Were you not happy in Florida last summer or were you not happy in the Michel Roux restaurant last week when we had that amazing meal? Or were you not happy when we went two months ago to the Brit Awards and were sitting in the VIP section? Which of these things didn't make you happy?"

"I am talking about feelings here, not about money!" Ralph's speech became stern. His previous comments had been made in a soft voice, the one he used every day. This tone was what had made him so popular among friends and business clients. He didn't have many social skills but he did have a very nice way of approaching people and it was easy to be around him. This time he used his 'other' approach. The one he did not exercise often but which was necessary when he dealt with Sam.

"Feelings! What feelings are you after? What feelings are you missing? What more can I give you?!"

"That is the problem, Sam. You cannot give me anything more. And I need more. I would like from life things I will never be able to experience here. In this house. With you."

"Are you having an affair?" Sam's face looked puzzled. For the first time in her life she did not know how to behave or what to say. She didn't know how to manipulate Ralph into what she wanted and she couldn't understand why. She had managed him so well for all these years.

Ralph didn't answer her question immediately. He just nervously swallowed. He looked very fragile, like a person who had not slept in a while. At the same time he was coming across as determined, which scared Sam. She simply didn't realize that getting to the point he was at had taken him many years and although it was exhausting, he had already decided.

"No, I did not have an affair. But I was thinking of one. There is this new architectural assistant in the office. A gay guy..."

Sam looked at Ralph with a sense of curiosity. Her eyes were wide open and on her face there seem to be expression of a surprise or rather shock.

"No, it is not what you think," Ralph laughed nervously, "I am not gay. Just this man, Andy, he lives with his boyfriend of a few years. And every day when we go for a cigarette he tells me some stories about their life. They seem to be very much in love with each other and despite years passing, they do things together. And they enjoy it. I can hear Andy on the phone to him. They often talk about various things but whatever the conversation is about, heavy or light, there is something in the air. Something that you can detect and that makes you understand how much is between them. Something that I have never experienced. We never do things together. We actually never see each other. You socialize with your friends and I socialize with mine. You go to the gym on different days than I do. You are not interested in my hobbies and never want to share anything about what you are passionate about. I feel that I am living next to you, not with you..." Ralph paused and took a deep breath. "I want to be like Andy. I want to feel that at home there is this special woman waiting for me. Or me waiting for her. I want us to laugh, to experience, to argue. But I want to feel about her the way Andy feels about his partner."

"Ralph, you are simply having a midlife crisis," said Sam decisively and she laughed strangely.

"No, it is not a crisis, Sam. I have been thinking for years about leaving. I don't like our life, the house we are living in and everything we do..."

"We can change it all. Today, whatever you want..." Sam sounded desperate.

"Sam, you don't get it although I tried to spare you this. I do not like any of this because I do not like it *with you*!" Ralph pronounced the last two words very strongly.

Sam was sitting there holding her hands on her knees. She looked like she had lost all this hyper energy which had been running their lives for the past nine years.

After a few minutes of silence, she straightened her body again and looked into Ralph's eyes.

"It is a shame that not much can be done…" Her head was high and she pushed her lips out.

"What do you mean, not much can be done?" Ralph responded not believing in what he had heard.

"There is nothing we can do about it. We have two children – we have to stay together for them. You cannot break up their family home."

"Sam, I am not breaking anything up. I am doing this as much for them as for myself. I would like them to get a different view of what adult life is like and what it should be like. I would like them to see us…me happy. And by being happy, I can be a better father and a better person. I want them to be able to see it." Ralph spoke with passion and conviction.

"So you suggest a divorce… Do you actually know what that means in this country? I mean," Sam corrected herself, "what it means to a man?"

Ralph didn't know what she was talking about. He looked at her like she was a creature from a different world.

"What are you talking about, Sam? It is the twenty-first century. Divorce is a normal thing. Many people get divorced."

"I didn't mean that. I meant the financial side of it."

"What financial side? You will get half of the value of the house and I will pay for the children until they are eighteen. I also will give you some money so that you can look for a job without any pressure. I will not hurt you…"

"You do not understand a thing, Ralph, do you? You have always been so naïve. I will not accept half of the house. I will not give you a divorce unless…I get the house and all of its contents. I also want a 'salary' for life and some other security...preferably shares in your company... Yes, half of the shares of your company exactly... And I will get this and even more as we have two children and the children's place is with their mother. And the courts in this country like people like me – full-time mothers who sacrifice their time in order to give the best to their children. They also hate people like you – successful, loaded men who break homes and leave their families behind. And who sooner or later start living in their riverside flash-pads with their new partners."

Ralph looked at her with astonishment. Over the years he'd understood that the Sam he had met and the Sam he lived with were two different people. He could see her becoming shrewd during their time together. He had witnessed her transformation from a quiet and modest person to rather loud and overconfident. What he saw now, however, was terrifying. She was not only greedy. She was calculated and evil. Ralph understood at that moment that this was who she was and that she hadn't changed, she just acted well when they had met.

"I will take you to court, Sam, and I will fight. There is no way you will get everything I worked for and there is no chance I will agree to you having part of the company which my father built for so many years. The courts may not be sympathetic towards men but they will find the difference between what is fair and what is sheer madness. And if you would like me to go down this path, I will. I cannot live like this any longer." Ralph was determined and left Sam in no doubt as to which way to go next.

"The court you are talking about may rule either way but the time you will lose without seeing your children, during these few years of the fight, will be years you will never be able to rebuild." Sam looked at Ralph with eyes that could kill. She also blushed; her faced was literally bright red. She knew that it wasn't yet another fight. She was about to start a war.

"What are you talking about? I will be seeing them as much as my work allows me and will take them to my place at least a few nights a week. Ideally, we would look after them in equal shares."

"I will not let you see them. And I am their mother and I can do it as children always stay with mothers. Yes, you can go to the family court and you may get one weekend every two weeks with them but that is as far as it can go. Have you heard about many men winning custody cases against women? I would have to murder one of them, so that you could get the custody of the other one... And it will take you years to get even there. In the meantime I will portray you as a bad father who doesn't come here to see his children. I will also contact everyone and I *mean* everyone to explain to them that you want to move me to a council house. That you want to leave me and the children without any sufficient means of living. How would your friends react to it? What would your clients say? Who do you think they would believe? You – a man who moves out from his family, away from his children, or me – a faithful wife who always stood behind her husband and who wasted her career in order to bring them up?"

Ralph was speechless. He always knew that she didn't care about their children. That she didn't like to spend any time with them. When she was at home, the children would be in their rooms. She never played with them nor cooked for them. Their housekeeper – a Russian au pair, Olga – was the one who not only cleaned and cooked but also helped the children with their homework, drew with them and chased them around the garden.

The fact that Sam might have used their children, despite the lack of love and attention towards them, was a painful discovery. Ralph adored his children and the thought that this was the person who was going to bring them up if he moved out was breaking his heart. He intended to move out on that night but he could not do it in these circumstances.

The following day Ralph went to work. He was thinking overnight and had decided to proceed with the divorce as he planned. He could not stand the thought of living with Sam before but now, after their conversation, even looking into her face filled him with dread. One of his friends recommended a solicitor to him, one who knew similar cases and was good at reaching satisfying settlements. And Ralph was full of hope. He decided to stay in the house for some time and to pretend in front of Sam that nothing had changed and that her threat had been successful. He smiled, he ate dinners with her, he even watched TV with her when the kids went to bed. But in the meantime he was arming himself for the clash which was yet to come. He transferred most of their liquid assets to his private bank accounts, cashing in others. Ralph also began to move his various documents out of the study in the house to his office. At the same time he hired a private detective who was keeping track of Sam and monitoring whether she had had similar ideas to him.

One day, four months later, the post arrived. Olga, as usual, collected all the letters from the hallway floor and placed them on the kitchen surface. She woke the children up and started making breakfast. Sam got up soon afterwards and was in a very bad mood. Olga knew that it was better not to approach her employer early in the morning. As a result of the previous night's drinking, Sam was always very tired and abrupt in the morning. Olga saw Sam sitting on the high stool by the kitchen island, in her usual habit, opening the post at the same time. Suddenly Olga heard a scream and turned towards Sam, only to witness a cup of coffee being thrown towards the wall. It smashed completely and the coffee was now dripping off the custom-made Italian tiles. Then Sam ran out of the house and jumped into her car. Olga could hear her screams from inside of the car and saw her hitting the steering wheel with her hands many times. She felt anxious whether the kids could hear it but she was even more curious about what was in the letter which had caused Sam's anger. She walked towards the chair previously occupied by Sam and picked the piece of paper from the stool. It was a letter from the court to which there was included a divorce petition. There was also another piece of paper saying something about social workers which Olga could not understand at all. She didn't want to know more anyway. It was beyond her understanding how someone like Ralph could be with Sam. He was so clever and sophisticated. He was also good to his sons and, unlike his wife, he never shouted at them.

Olga always felt that Ralph should leave Sam and find someone else. Someone who would give him a real home. A home with love and respect. This person should also care for his children and treat them like they were her own. At least until they would be sent off to boarding school. Olga had liked Ralph for a very long time and now she thought that there could be a chance for them to be together. She was young, pretty and well educated. She could do everything a woman should be able to do but at the same time she had a heart. They could be a perfect couple, Olga thought. She also thought that she could look after this amazing house so much better than Sam. Yes, Olga could see herself as a mistress of this mansion. She could see herself throwing big parties during which she would be wearing nice clothes and jewellery. She would have many new friends she could meet at the local golf club every day, when Ralph would be at work. But she would be kind and gracious and friendly. And she would have a housekeeper too. Just like herself. Someone who could do everything in the house so that she could start enjoying herself. After all, everyone deserves a good life…

Californian Dream

I was in the cab. The motorway we were on was of gigantic proportions, like ones you can see only in America. The landscape was rather sleepy with an endless sea of cars passing in all directions. I felt like I was in a desert – the sun was shining with persistent strength and the metallic surfaces of the surrounding vehicles were giving an effect similar to the one experienced by people witnessing a *Fata Morgana*. I was tired, worn out and not looking forward to the next few days.

As a journalist, I was used to travelling but this trip was different. My assignment did not present the intellectual challenges I was accustomed to but it was well paid. Having an ex-wife and a seven-year-old son taught me to undertake any job which gave sufficiently high financial rewards. Such as this one. Over the course of the last few months I did not reject any job offers. This attitude kept me away from my best friend since the divorce – alcohol. I hadn't touched it for seventy-three days and nine hours. It was difficult to resist it in the crammed Virgin plane, with a passenger in front of me lowering his seat to such a level that he was practically sleeping on my lap (had they shrunk these planes over the last few years?). It felt extremely claustrophobic and an uncooperative steward did not allow me to walk when others were sleeping, claiming that it was dangerous in case we had turbulence. I have never been massively fond of flying but changes in recent years, resulting in painfully overcrowded planes, airport staff treating passengers like savages and frustrated and patronizing flight attendants had turned my dislike of flying into a deeply grounded and irreversible hatred. Despite the situation on the plane I decided to stick to my decision of remaining sober and, instead of drinking, I chewed two packs of mint gum over the thirteen-hour flight.

I have visited LA several times before. In my old life – before the divorce – and in my new one: the one of a middle-aged man who, at all cost tries to fight back all the signs of approaching forty. Not many people like Los Angeles – most European tourists prefer staying in San Francisco or going to Carmel. But I have always liked this place. A rough and socially diverse town presented endless research opportunities for a journalist who liked social experiments. This time, however, I did not come here as a journalist…not a real one, at least. I was sent to America in order to conduct an interview with Galvo, a star of one of the most popular reality TV shows.

Due to the generosity of my employer, a colourful weekly gossip magazine, I had a room in the Vice President Hotel in Santa Monica. An ugly tower block from outside, inside was one of the trendiest and most fashionable hotels to stay in. I did like it, despite the small rooms and noisy corridors. It was urban, chic, non-pretentious and allowed for a quick walk down the hill to the ocean. My visit was planned for three days but, despite the ample time, I knew I wasn't going to have much of it for myself. American celebrities like being the centre of attention and I was expecting that after the first meeting I would be called back to ask some additional questions, or at least our photographer would be. In the end, there was nothing more important than looking good on the cover of a gossipy magazine.

We seemed to be driving for hours. I checked my watch – my head was still working on European time. In London it was already the middle of the night but here it was the peak of rush hour. I felt bored and quite negative about everything I could see. Undoubtedly, I was tired and I deserved a bath and bed.

Three hours later I felt much better. Refreshed by a proper clean-up and a short nap I could face the world again. My mobile rang:

"Hello, old Devil!" I heard on the phone.

"Tracy! How amazing to hear your voice!" I said with genuine excitement. We were childhood friends and stayed in touch over the past nearly thirty years, on and off. We corresponded over our boarding school time, university and later in adult life. We had seen each other occasionally at various weddings of shared friends and later, when my paediatrician wife was working in the same hospital as Tracy's husband Lars, a Swedish surgeon, the four of us went out once or twice a year. Last year Lars and Tracy moved to LA where he became the head of a well-known Beverly Hills clinic.

"You promised to call me from the airport! How was your flight?"

"Dull and horrid," I said in a childlike manner. I knew that I still could be charming and funny in a Hugh-Grant manner and I wanted to flirt with Tracy. We both liked doing this, having no intention of going any further with it. We had a lot of shared past and were at the stage where neither of us felt obliged to pretend anything to the other one.

"Good, after the way you treat me that was all you deserved!" She decided to speak like a little girl too.

"Could you find any time for me? I should have the next two evenings free. My interview with Galvo is scheduled for tomorrow at eleven in the morning and I hope he will not give me too much of a hard time." We both laughed, knowing how famously unpredictable Galvo could be.

"I admire you. After all the great interviews with real people you have done, you decided to do this piece...as well." She was joking but I also sensed in her voice an element of genuine surprise. It sounded like disappointment, or maybe that was the way I felt about it.

"You know, darling, that some of us have mortgages to pay off, ex-wives and real life responsibilities..."

"Blah, blah, blah, I won't give you any opportunity to pity yourself. You are a grown man and you choose what you do..."

"It may look that way from the perspective of a stay-at-home wife with a surgeon husband earning a seven-figure salary every year..." I said it in a soft manner, in the way we mocked each other all the time.

"You are impossible and if you don't stop patronizing me I will come to your hotel and slap you across that pretty face of yours."

"Oh, yes...please," we were back to our semi-vulgar jokes.

We both laughed. It was good to feel at ease with someone especially the day before a very staged and superficial, as I predicted, interview.

"I will always find time for you, darling. When could we have the pleasure of hosting you?" Tracy was back in her motherly spirit, when one feels the need to clothe, feed and entertain every stranger only because he seems to be accidentally passing by.

"I should have the evening off tomorrow. Could this work for you?" I answered cooperatively.

"Sounds perfect. I will throw a little party. You, Lars, me and Cheryl with her husband…"

"What Cheryl? Who the fuck is Cheryl?" Tracy had a very English habit of throwing into a conversation names of people one had never heard of before and making it like this person was a well-known and familiar figure.

"She is my neighbour…my friend…my spiritual guide…" This last one was said with a grave seriousness mixed with exaltation.

"I will gladly meet every Tom, Dick and Harry, as long as the dinner is tasty and you provide me with a lot of still water…"

"Christ! How boring… I forgot you are sober now through and through…we will have to make you have some fun whether you like it or not… Could you be here at seven… or let's say seven thirty? I forgot that Cheryl is doing her healing classes until seven fifteen…"

"I will be there with a British punctuality."

"In that case I will see you tomorrow. *Adieu, mon ami…*" and she put the phone down without waiting for my response.

It was good to hear Tracy's voice. She has always had a very grounding effect on me and the entire surreal aim of my American journey became much less painful as a result. Galvo may waffle about whatever he wanted but then I could just descend from the high hills of Beverly Hills to a much more normal environment with my old childhood friend.

There was light at the end of the tunnel.

The phone rang. The receptionist on the other side put me through to Corina, Galvo's agent, and we confirmed the precise time of the interview. She also took from me an order for my lunch, which I was supposed to eat in the company of the teenage reality-show icon.

I went to the gym, then had a quick swim and went out to the little restaurant round the corner. The place looked like a Manhattan loft-turned-restaurant and was very dark, which stood in a sharp contrast to the quite sleepy and endlessly sunny Santa Monica. After eating only a small part of my Caesar salad – the entire portion could have fed an army – I went for a walk along the ocean. The sea with its regular waves had always had a very calming effect on me. It also allowed me to put to sleep a sudden need for a glass of bourbon, which had dominated all my thoughts over dinner.

I got back to my room, set the alarm clock and went to bed with the latest biography of Giuseppe Tomasi di Lampedusa. This was always my favourite pastime: lying in comfortable bed linens with a good book and a glass of bourbon. Recently a cup of herbal tea had to do for me instead. Initially, I was reading with a hope that I would fall asleep, like it happened normally at home. That night I could not sleep at all; maybe it was jet lag or maybe the urge for alcohol but I could not find my peace. Eventually when the sun was already rising I managed to fall into a slow, foggy and rather light doze which as soon as it began to relax me was cut by the sharp and brutal signal of my alarm. I must have slept for at least three hours but I felt like it was ten, maybe fifteen minutes. I got up heavy and tired. I picked up the book, which had rolled down to the floor over night. I went to the bathroom and took a shower after which I ordered some fruit to my room and logged on to my computer. I wanted to revise all my knowledge about Galvo and his world: with his several plastic surgeries, four houses and seventy-eight million-dollar net worth.

The car, with a large Afro-American driver, was waiting in front of the hotel punctually at nine forty-five. Initially we were driving alongside the beaches of Santa Monica and the ocean, only to turn right cutting through the rough and unwelcoming heart of Los Angeles, to then find ourselves in the hills, again in the oasis of peace, wealth and luxury. Galvo's house was located in a type of gated development which contained yet more fences and gates within. Each house was surrounded by its own high fence, on top of the one wrapping the entire development. Galvo's house – to my surprise – was in the style of a southern plantation with eight large pillars holding the roof of a wide veranda. Despite the fact that it was out of place, it seemed far too classy and stylish for everything I knew and expected about Galvo.

As soon as the car parked in front of the main entrance, the door opened and the well-known figure of Galvo came out with his arms widely open.

"I have heard so much about you! As a teenager I loved reading your short stories in the *New Yorker* and I have read both your books. I hope you don't mind that I requested you?" Galvo said it all in one breath, overwhelming me both with the intensity of our meeting but also with the fact that he possibly knew as much about me as I did about him.

"I am honoured." It was a bit clumsy as I was still getting out of the car. "I am very pleased to meet you," I repeated, with more belief in my words.

He led me up the stairs and through the long hallway, cutting the house in half, to the door on the other side, which led to the gardens. By the swimming pool there was a large white canopy tent set up with comfortable cushions, a table for two and many trestle tables containing various crystal decanters and fruit bowls.

"It is beautiful," I said loudly, showing my surprise not only with the grand lifestyle of Galvo but more with the stylishness of the entire set-up. It was not the house of a person who calls his mother a blue-blood whore on TV or who feeds the public around the world with the details of his sex orgies. This was a house of someone with refined means, good taste and certain level of sensitivity – from the open French windows of the mansion I could hear the first piano concerto of Chopin.

I sat comfortably on one of the garden sofas and smiled politely at Galvo. He clearly could see that I was impressed.

"You have a beautiful house. I read somewhere that you bought it off people who had no intention of selling but your offer was too generous to refuse..."

"I read that too. Very interesting fairy tale," Galvo responded promptly.

We both laughed – him naturally, me more as a result of a need to fit into the situation.

"When can we start?" I asked taking a sip of water from the glass placed by my side by the butler.

"Haven't we started already?" Galvo smiled at me again.

I placed an extra cushion behind my back. Galvo was looking at me with his shining eyes, like he was expecting a punch and was ready to take it.

"Let's start with your childhood. There are various

stories about your parents' wealth – you yourself stated several times how comfortable your childhood was – nevertheless, no one can find any traces of a family fortune. Your mother was a legal clerk, yes, from an old southern family, but of very low income herself while your father was not even registered at your birth. Where are you really from, Galvo?"

He looked at me with disappointment but soon his well-trained public face was again on display.

"I have to be honest, I was hoping that you would be more interested in finding out about me and my intellectual side, rather than repeating common gossip. With your past and career there are so many more interesting questions one could start from..."

"I am sure you understand that there is a certain group of readers who buy the magazine and I am not sure if your thoughts regarding Jean-Paul Sartre would mean much to them," I smiled, with an effort to mask the affront to my first question.

"I know what is the profile of your magazine... Only, after all these years of giving interviews to the gossip press, I was hoping that by choosing you I would finally get to meet someone who would be interested not in Galvo but in me..." He laughed artificially.

"But Galvo is you...isn't it the person who produces his own show, who pays cheques to dozens of people working for him? Isn't it Galvo who created the image of a celebrity spoiled brat, a male version of Paris Hilton? This is the person people watch on TV and whose life they would like to read about. Why is he so moody? Where does his money really come from? Does he really take a bath in sheep's milk every morning?" I heard myself and hated what I was saying.

"Galvo, there is a phone call for you," a voice from inside the house shouted.

"You will have to excuse me," he said to me with additional courtesy and walked towards the open French windows.

I felt very low, like a person who betrayed everything he believed in. Was I really this type of journalist? Is it really who I'd become? Was it because of the money, or maybe, despite all my intellectual pretentions, I was a part of a shallow and washed-out mass culture?

Galvo was running towards me.

"I am very sorry but we will have to reschedule the interview. I will have to leave now. My driver will take you back to your hotel. I promise to find some time for you tomorrow, any time which suits you really…" And he left me there on my own.

On my way to the hotel I was thinking about my stupid question and the explanation afterwards. I wanted to call him and apologize. I wanted to do something to make him feel differently about me or maybe to make me think differently about myself.

In the lobby of the hotel I recognized the familiar figure of Tracy. Only about fifty pounds heavier than I remembered.

"I thought I would come to say hello before your interview and ask if you need picking up tonight," she said giving me kisses on each of my cheeks. "I wasn't sure what time you would be here…"

"I have already been to the interview but it was postponed till tomorrow," I said still thinking about the impression I made and not acknowledging fully Tracy's presence.

"Obviously that is Galvo for you…" There was something nasty in Tracy's voice.

"No…not at all, it wasn't that. Something happened… I don't know really what… It was strange…he was strange…"

"I know, he is completely bonkers, everyone knows that…"

"No," I said again, but this time in a much stronger voice, "he is not the way he shows himself to people. There is another side to him, a different, intellectual edge…"

"Intellectual edge? You must have met someone else rather than Galvo then," Tracy said with confidence. "It is good to see you and you look fantastic," she added.

I didn't know what to say as clearly I could not honestly complement her looks. Looking at her now again I realized that not only had she put on weight but also she didn't seem to care about herself the way she used to…the way I remembered.

"You know what?" I said suddenly surprising even myself. "I had an awful morning. What are you doing today? Shall we start our party now? I could take you for lunch and we could take it from there?"

"I have a better idea," Tracy responded spontaneously, "let's go to mine now. We can swim in the pool, chat and enjoy the sun. Like there was no tomorrow!"

"Deal!"

Tracy put her hand into mine and we left the hotel. We waited for a few minutes for the valet who was about to bring the car and despite the obvious sign prohibiting smoking, we both smoked two cigarettes each. We were chatting about our old friends, about my ex-wife, who Tracy never liked and used to call 'Hermenegilde', referring possibly to her harsh manner of speaking and German origins. Eventually we got into the car and were driving slowly through the sunny broad roads of Santa Monica. It was very hot, but the light breeze from the Pacific made it not only bearable but rather pleasurable. Tracy didn't speak for a while. She was only smoking – her fourth cigarette since we left the Vice President – and staring blindly in front of her.

"How are things, Tracy? How are the children? How is Lars?" I asked feeling that the silence had made things rather tense and uncomfortable.

"Great, all is great!" she smiled and carried on staring at the road.

"Do you enjoy living here?"

"What is there not to enjoy? The sun, the big house with a swimming pool, exciting, flashy parties..." She paused for a while, took a deep breath and started smoking another cigarette. "The truth is," she began again, "that I hate it. I cannot stand how thick people are and I am sick of looking at the world through American eyes. Here, everything is about the money. People are only interesting if they are rich, even if they have nothing to say. I feel lonely and I would possibly be back in England by now if not for...Cheryl."

I was taken aback by Tracy's honesty. I didn't want to drill deeper to find out the real source of her frustration but at the same time I didn't want to leave the conversation at this point. We were friends and I couldn't feel indifferent about her genuine sadness.

"Are the kids finding it better? At least for them it must be a good, if somewhat challenging, experience?"

"Yes, you are absolutely right. It is very life-building for them: they meet people from around the world – the school is really good – and they love the weather. The boys took up surfing and Lavinia is thinking of an acting career, so she has started attending various castings for teenagers. I am not particularly happy about it but then it is better if she finds her own way in the world. Otherwise she may end up like me." Tracy turned her head towards me and there were tears in her eyes.

I looked over to her and made a grin with my lips showing a mix of understanding and pity. I did not know what to say.

We made a final turn and stopped in front of a large bungalow. It looked like it was from the 1920s – all in Spanish style with white-plastered arches and black steel arabesque gates.

Tracy jumped out of the car and opened her arms,

"Welcome to my home! If you live in California, you have to live in style. Doesn't everyone wish to live a Californian dream?" I wasn't sure if she was seriously proud or painfully sarcastic about the entire thing.

"It is beautiful, Tracy, really, how I would imagine your house would be," I responded.

"Come inside, we even have a pool which I heated up especially for you!"

We went through a large open-plan sitting room to a dark and shiny kitchen.

"What can I get for you? I have a homemade iced tea. Alcohol-free," Tracy winked.

"Can I have some then, please?"

"I will make it with a slice of fresh lemon and a handful of ice. It tastes best this way." Tracy seemed to be chattier than she had been before. "I hope you don't mind if I have something stronger...?"

"Of course not, Tracy. I have to pay for my old sins. No need for the entire world to live in purgatory," I smiled at her.

"So how is your life? I have been waffling about my spoiled selfish kids, careless and unfaithful partner and lonely depressing life in a country I hate but I haven't heard a word from you. About your life..." After this Tracy took a deep sip of drink.

There was a difficult pause.

"Tracy, I am so sorry... You haven't told me anything about Lars or the children... I thought you were only a bit down, you know, like people are, when they've had too much sun and not enough to do. How do you feel about it?" I asked, not understanding all the things she threw at me with such speed.

"How do I feel about what? About Lars shagging his nurses or about the kids who don't even care where I am as long as the dinner is there and the clean clothes are in their wardrobes? Or how do I feel hating the place I live in and not knowing how to get out of my depression? How do I feel about life? About aging? About getting fat thanks to the American super-size portions? How do I fell about what?!" The last question Tracy shouted out through tears of anger and tiredness.

I stood up from my chair and walked towards her standing by the kitchen island. I put my arms around her from behind her and leaned my chin on her arm.

"I didn't know you were so unhappy, as a matter of fact I didn't know you were unhappy at all. Let's fix drinks and talk in peace. You will tell me everything and I will listen... like an old friend who you will not see often enough to feel guilty about your honesty, like a person who will not judge you, having a past of his own."

She turned towards me and whispered, "I would like

that very much. It is so good to see you. I have been so lonely and..."

At this moment the outside door of her patio opened and a woman in her fifties marched into the room without invitation. She was wearing a jumpsuit, had a silk scarf on her head coming down to her neck where it was tied in a bow and she was wearing big sun glasses.

"Hello, darling! I have been longing to see you today! My last two clients were cancelled so I decided to pop in a bit earlier," as she was approaching Tracy, she noticed me in the corner of the L-shaped sitting room.

"Hello, Cheryl, you have to meet my old friend," Tracy said in a suddenly calm and quiet manner. "This is Nick... Nick, this is Cheryl. I told you that Cheryl is the only person who keeps me grounded here." They looked at each other and smiled. Cheryl nodded her head.

"She is actually very grounded herself, only sometimes she loses her objectives," Cheryl said like Tracy wasn't present in the room.

"I don't feel like I would like to cook today, Nick. Is it okay if we order a pizza for dinner?" Tracy said more telling me than really asking.

"I am just a guest. Please do whatever works for you. I don't mind pizza or indeed anything you order. As a matter of fact, I rather enjoy American food."

"Couldn't be better," Tracy responded. "I will go and place an order. Do you mind if I do ten minutes of meditation in my bedroom with Cheryl? It is so much better to do it now, before the kids come back home..."

"No, I will just go to the garden and relax for a few minutes. I feel very worn out today," I stated truthfully.

"You simply have to relax and switch off. You are now amongst friends," Cheryl stated in a calm but decisive manner. For a brief moment I felt like one of her clients.

I took my drink and went out through the garden door while Cheryl and Tracy went to the left side of the house where the bedrooms were situated. The entire building was surrounding a large courtyard with a tiled pool. The plants were growing alongside the chalk-white walls and blossoming with red and orange flowers. The day was immensely beautiful and, looking up at the blue sky lit purple by the sunset, one had to admire the film-like scenery. That was the reason why so many people loved California. With its space, exotic nature and endlessly blue sky, this place had all one could need to be happy. One could appreciate the beauty and marvel of the world, and gain distance from all problems: the darkness of family trauma, addictions or complexes. At that very moment, like so many others before me, I felt liberated by the tranquillity of the setting. I felt nearly happy.

I was walking alongside the pool, under the arches of the inner courtyard, passing by the long enfilade of bedrooms. In one of the windows I noticed Tracy's head. Out of sheer curiosity, I decided to come closer and put my head in, like a child, surprising all the people inside. As I was about to do it I saw Tracy and Cheryl sitting on the floor with a low coffee table between them both touching its surface. I came a few inches closer only to find Tracy moving her head across the table in a slow manner, inhaling something in front of her. She was breathing in heavily, with greed. As I understood what was happening in the room I pulled my head back, trying to avoid being noticed. It was an intimate moment and I wasn't meant to be a part of it. But it was too late. Cheryl looked into the window only to discover my embarrassed face there. To my surprise she didn't find looking into my eyes difficult. She straightened her neck and smiled towards me. It was a smile of someone who had won, someone who was in charge, someone who had an advantage over you. Cheryl had some sort of power over Tracy; it was noticeable now, very clearly, and she knew how to exercise it. I could not compete with that. Tracy was lying on the carpet slowly rubbing the top of her nose, helping the drug to spread more efficiently. At this moment I realized that I had lost her. She was no longer my friend Tracy, no longer the person I knew. She was now living in the world of Cheryl and people like her. Lost to whatever she had in front of herself. I felt confused – a real friend would approach her and attempt to talk to her, maybe even try to help her to cure the habit. I had experience of this, and I knew that there was nothing like recreational use of hard drugs, and that it always sooner or later ended up in the dark place. I also knew how difficult it was to break from the addiction. But I wasn't a real friend really. After all those years and with my past what right did I have to interfere in her life? To give her advice I could not support with any real help? And to be honest, I didn't lose her then. It happened a long time before and I had only lived with the image of someone who I once knew. I had changed since we were children and now I understood that so had Tracy. And it was her right to choose the path she wanted to take and my advice, no matter how non-judgemental, wasn't required.

I thought about what was to come the following day, about Galvo and our interview. Should I ask him the same questions I had prepared before or should I try to bring my real self to this job? Maybe I should ask him questions

I would ask heads of states or great philosophers, questions that really mattered to me and, as it seemed, to him. In the end, the interview didn't have to be published, or maybe it would and it could prove that people are not as infantile as journalists are trying to make them out to be. Maybe there are a few more people out there who would like to know what motivates someone like him to wake up every morning and to create one of the most hated and loved TV personalities of our times. And where does the boundary go? How does he know who he really is after all? Isn't it a question we all would like to know the answer to? Who we really are...?

I looked into the room again. Tracy was having her dream: maybe of a beautiful house, filled with a loving family. A dream of a happy self: slim, smiling, free from any addictions and anxieties. A dream of happiness under the Californian sun.

The Old Lady

Mary pressed the button. At first no one answered. Mary knew what to expect. Mrs Pamela Thyme-Leigh had told Mary a lot about her mother, Mary's new employer. Although, technically, Mrs Thyme-Leigh was her new employer as she was the one making the monthly transfers of Mary's salary.

The anxiety felt ever so present; despite everything that Mrs Thyme-Leigh had told Mary about the old lady, she felt that there was much more to the entire story than had been explained to her. Mary was also convinced that she didn't like Mrs Thyme-Leigh. It wasn't anything in particular; only somewhere, under the skin, Mary could detect her coldness and deep-seated class superiority, as there were no doubts about Mrs Thyme-Leigh's high social standing.

Mary looked around. Ecclestone Square, only a few minutes walk from Victoria Station, was one of those places which seemed to sink in a capsule of time. In the middle of it was a long rectangular private garden surrounded by high and narrow white stucco buildings. Her new employer's apartment was in one of those buildings and Mrs Thyme-Leigh had prepared Mary for a tiresome climb – it was on the third floor with no lift.

"H...hello?" the voice coming from the speaker seemed to be very tired.

"It is Mary, madam, your new nurse..."

"I do not expect a nurse..."

The accent of the old lady was very strong and foreign. Eastern European, maybe Russian, Mary thought. She understood now why the day before she found the surname of Mrs Thyme-Leigh's mother unpronounceable. Initially, she just thought it was very posh, just like Mrs Thyme-Leigh herself. Now she knew it was also foreign.

"I was employed by your daughter, madam..."

"I do not maintain any relationships with my daughter, so it must be some sort of mistake. Please leave."

The pitch of the old lady was low, yet very strong and powerful. It was a tone in which you give orders which others are supposed to obey. For a brief moment Mary thought about leaving but then she reminded herself about the handsome cheque from Mrs Thyme-Leigh and decided to press the button again. The same voice answered.

"Who is it?!" This time it sounded even more abrupt and irritated.

"It is Mary Johnson. I am your new nurse and I would like to enter your apartment, madam. Otherwise I will have to call an ambulance, suspecting that you may be unwell..."

There was a pause on the other side. Mary knew well, from her own experience, that old people, just like children, were petrified of the thought of being taken to the hospital.

The door buzzed and Mary decisively pushed it forward. The lobby was very spacious but its best days were long gone. It was very clean, but more like pensioners' homes are rather than apartment buildings in a fashionable part of London with the sky-high prices. On the left hand side of the entrance there were the post boxes of all the occupiers with their surnames on. Mary read them through. A few cards were with double-barrelled names, just like Mrs Thyme-Leigh. Several surnames had various titles before them such as Dr This and Capt. That. One of them caught her attention: Sir James Colthorpe.

Mary thought that it must be nice to wake up in the morning and think, I am Sir James Colthorpe, how shall I spend my day? Or maybe let's just save it for a change. She laughed to herself. Mary remembered this quote from the favourite book of her mother, *The Age of Innocence*. She was made to read it as a teenager and it was chasing her in her nightmares until that day. Mary giggled again. This world was just as old-fashioned as the world of May Welland and Newland Archer. She was already on the second floor. All the doors to the apartments she passed by were made of heavy wood with various gold decorations. Everything was very luxurious and she felt slightly insecure walking in her boots on the soft cream carpets. It was smart but with a deep need of a coat of fresh paint. Mary instantly disliked the ambience of her new workplace.

She got to the third floor. The door in front of her was slightly ajar. She walked in and found herself in a round vestibule. The walls were in a pink colour and alongside their curved shapes there were chairs with a stripy grey fabric. It was very grand.

"Come in. I won't bite..." she heard from the room to the left hand side of the hallway. Mary carefully closed the door and took her shoes off, leaving her coat on the metal shabby chic rack.

Mary walked into a spacious square-shaped corner room. It had four windows, two on each of the external walls. Inside there was a large fireplace, at least half a dozen armchairs, a grand piano, numerous tables, several lamps and rugs. The walls were decorated with striped wallpaper. Strangely, despite the clutter, it all worked together and the room was very cosy and pleasant, which automatically put Mary at ease. At the very end of the room she noticed a big wing armchair occupied by an old woman. A very old woman.

"Come closer, so that I can look at you. At my age my sight is not what it used to be anymore…" Mary heard from the corner of the room.

Mary walked towards the woman,

"I am Mary Johnson. It is very nice to meet you." She wanted to shake hands with her new employer but the cold look she felt from the old lady stopped her from making this attempt.

"I do admire your wit. I bet that the threat of a hospital works on all old people like myself." She looked towards the window.

The old lady was very slim and her fitted suit made her look even slimmer. Her neck was tied with a soft and colourful scarf with a big green and gold brooch. Mary thought this is how real emeralds must look. Her new patient seemed to have lots of inner energy but this was trapped in her disabled body. With her sharp aristocratic jaw and bony hands she looked like a beautiful bird which had broken its wing. The old woman gave the impression of a fragile person held together only by the strength of will and stubbornness.

"I am sorry for using this trick, madam," Mary decided

to be honest, "but I really wanted to see you. I believe I could be a help to you and that, after you meet me, you may decide to keep me."

"I thought you said it is already decided. That my daughter is paying you... We old people are treated like children in these days and there is not much one can do about it at my age..."

"Your daughter hired me, madam, but I can't be here against your will."

Mary was surprised by the intelligence of the old lady. Not that she thought that old people couldn't be intelligent. It was, however, unusual for many of them to be so sharp in their thoughts and to express themselves in such a clear manner. And Mary had looked after very many old people before. Mrs Thyme-Leigh had told her that the lady was in her late nineties so the lively conversation which they just had came to Mary as a surprise.

"So do they expect me to die soon?" the old woman asked.

"No, they just would like to know that you are not on your own."

"I have been on my own for the last thirty-something years. And I didn't miss any of them. Did you hear me – *any*!" The last phrase she shouted.

Mary had been told by Mrs Thyme-Leigh about the difficult family relationships. She didn't go into too much detail and Mary didn't know whether it was appropriate to show any of her knowledge now.

"How old are you?" The last question was asked in a kind and calm tone. Mary was taken aback by this. She was already thinking about a way of unloading the bad temper of her future patient, not suspecting that the old lady would do the work herself.

"Twenty-seven." Mary always answered questions using the minimum number of words.

"Are you from London?" The old lady seemed to be inquisitive but at her age those questions didn't come across as tactless.

"No, I grew up in the Midlands but went to the University of Brighton. This is my second year in London."

"I have been here since 1946. Wretched town. Everyone seems to be busy all the time here. People run somewhere but they can't really tell you where it is. Nor do they know what they are after."

"And where did you live before, madam?" Mary felt it was a long shot but she simply tried to find a connection with the woman. However, as soon as she asked the question she realized that it wasn't right. The old woman became once again stern and serious and looked towards the window. The only difference was that now it seemed like she could see her past there.

"No one has really asked me this question for years. People think that it is better not to. That an old person may not to want to talk about the time when one was young. But the truth is, I long to talk about it. And the older I am, the desire to dwell on it is stronger." She paused for a while. Her right hand touched her ear, in a gesture which seemed to be checking whether a pearl stud-earring was still there. She took a deep breath in and when she breathed out her head shook slightly, like people with Parkinson's disease.

"I was born in Prague. Although today it is in the Czech Republic, then it was still a part of an Austro-Hungarian empire. My mother died in childbirth. My father was an officer in the Austrian army. He took rather badly the collapse of the empire and the fact that with the end of the Great War, which you call now the World War One, his country ceased to exist. He drank himself to death. Literally. I can hardly remember what he looked like. I grew up with relatives. Very kind people but they couldn't create a home for me, so they sent me to a convent school with boarding. I didn't really care much for the education as I wanted to be a ballet dancer. I was practicing for hours, every day, endlessly. But they didn't allow me. I was married off as soon as I completed my schooling at the age of eighteen to a German landowner in the Czech part of Silesia. I didn't love my first husband but back then, in our social circle, there were only very few people who married for love. The war came but to us not much had changed. We were away from the front lines and our life was, really, quite idyllic. The estate was vast and the house always full of the friends and family of my husband. We had a daughter. Despite the family I never ceased dreaming about a career as a dancer and I still practiced daily. After all I was only in my early twenties... Are you paying attention?"

"Yes, I am sorry I was just checking my phone...whether I received a message from my other patient." Mary blushed knowing that it was a text from Chris, a man she met last week, she was looking for.

"I am not used to being interrupted."

"I am really sorry...and what happened next?"

"Nothing. The war ended and I moved to London." The old lady quite visibly lost interest in her story. Or maybe she just didn't want to tell it to Mary anymore.

"But what happened to your husband and your daughter?

Is this Mrs Thyme-Leigh?" Mary, feeling guilty, desperately tried to make her patient go back to the conversation.

The old woman looked distant now. She seemed to be looking somewhere on the far side of the room but her mind wasn't there. It was again searching for something seventy years before, there, in Eastern Europe.

"No, I had the daughter you mentioned here in London, after I moved to Britain."

She paused again and suddenly continued her previously interrupted story, just like nothing had happened in the meantime. Like she had forgotten she got annoyed with Mary for not listening to her.

"The Germans were losing the war. And my husband was a German. I was one too because I married him. At the end of 1944 the Soviets were approaching and our peaceful little heaven very quickly turned into a river full of people who had to escape their homes in the east. We tried to help them but the house was soon full and unlimited – till then – supplies of food ceased. We had more people than we could feed. With the hunger a fear came as those who managed to escape the Red Army brought gruesome stories of the unspeakable cruelty of our approaching enemy. One day I received a message that the army hospital in which my husband was recuperating after being injured in action on the Eastern Front was captured by the Soviets. My husband with other patients was dragged out from his bed and brutally murdered. It wasn't a shock. He was in the army for quite a few years by then and in the war husbands were dying all the time. Those husbands who were loved, alongside the unloved ones. I felt only sorry for my little daughter who would never remember her father."

"I am really sorry, it must have…" Mary tried to express how this sudden and unexpected wave of honesty from the old lady made her feel sympathetic towards her. She could feel that her coldness was only a mask helping her to deal with the gravity of what she was saying. But she wasn't allowed to speak and the old woman carried on with her monologue, not noticing Mary's attempts.

"My daughter was three and I knew I had to do something. And the only way seemed to be by escaping towards the West. But Hitler didn't allow anyone to escape, in the fear that this could demoralize the rest of his Reich. And one afternoon the Soviets entered our house. I was upstairs and saw on the ground floor landing soldiers dragging our young cook by her hair to the courtyard. I heard screams of women around the ground floor of the house and the noise of broken glass everywhere. It was like witnessing the judgement day. And they saw me. Two of them were running up the stairs and I felt frozen in fear. They hit me in my face and immediately pushed me to the floor. First to rape me was the officer. The next one was his soldier. They were very brutal and while doing this, they were also hitting me. I felt that my body was separating from my mind. And at a certain point I didn't feel anything anymore. Until I saw behind them my daughter holding her teddy and crying…"

Mary's eyes were full of tears but the eyes of the old woman were dry and her face did not show any signs of emotion. She was like an ancient sculpture, with no expression.

"The rapes continued for the next week. The soldiers were coming and going. Day. Night. Endlessly. Most of the women did not care and when they saw them approaching they were just lying down in order to avoid a beating. And we were all equal then: peasant women, domestic servants or women of my standing. We all knew what was done to us and we thought that this is how it was going to be to the end of our lives.

"But one day Soviets entered the house again. This time they left us in peace, taking all the children. It was winter and they took them the way they were in the house. Without any coats, sometimes without any shoes. We all saw them marching towards the fields. In deep snow. Barefoot. Some women were crying, others were screaming and hitting the soldiers. I stood still. I did not want to give them any moral satisfaction. I did not say a word. And I have not seen my daughter since... I did not say a word..."

The old lady turned her face towards Mary and her lower lip was shaking. Mary was crying and didn't know what to say. The old woman spoke again.

"Now, when you see what a monster I am, could you ever look into my face again?"

Mary didn't say a word; she just approached her employer and took her right hand into hers. They sat like this for some time. In complete silence. One next to another, in a mutual understanding that only women can have between each other. Mary knew that she was going to stay. She also knew that the old lady would not like her on the following day anymore, feeling guilty for this unusual moment of frankness. But Mary wanted to be there. Not for the lady but for herself.

Mary looked out of the window. She could see the tops of the trees growing in the communal garden and could hear the birds singing. Builders on the scaffolding, assembled on the other side of the square, were shouting loudly to each other in a foreign language. And a woman with a little child was walking along the road. They stopped by the traffic lights. The child looked up to the woman and stretched its hand towards her. She grabbed it, said something to the child and they crossed together.

The Solar Eclipse

"Thomas, do you know that today there is going to be a solar eclipse? Miss da Silva at school said it will be the last one for seventy-five years. Thomas, how old will you be when the next solar eclipse happens?" Sophie, my eight-year-old stepdaughter, flooded me with questions when I was driving her to school.

"You tell me, Clever Turtle," I responded, calling her by the nickname I gave her years ago, which she seemed to enjoy ever since.

"Right... You are now thirty-four..."

"Thirty-three!" I corrected her. She always tried to add some years in order to tease me.

"You are now thirty-three," she started again, smiling, showing many gaps in between her healthy white teeth, "so I would have to add to it seventy-five..."

"So how old will I be?"

"Wait... I am counting." She was puzzled. "You are going to be...hundred...hundred and seven...a hundred and seven!" Now Sophie was certain.

"Are you sure?" I asked.

"I am...a hundred and fifty per cent!"

"I am afraid it is not the right answer..." I upset her by

saying this. She pulled her lips down and looked through the window.

"Shall we try again?" I asked her. So we did and we counted together until we got to the right number. Soon afterwards Sophie started again,

"So if you are going to be a hundred and eight," she thought aloud, "are you going to be alive then?"

I laughed:

"I don't know, Clever Turtle. I have a slight chance. You know that everyone in my family lives to a very old age. My grandmother is turning ninety-eight this year, so who knows what may happen in seventy-five years to me?"

"I am going to be eighty-three!" Sophie already forgot about me and her inquisitive question, focusing the conversation characteristically on herself, "and I definitely will be alive. Mummy's mum lived to that age…"

She paused for a few seconds,

"Thomas, do you remember where you were when the last eclipse happened? I wasn't born then! I wasn't even in my mummy's belly then! Last night on TV I heard that it was fifteen years ago…"

As a matter of fact I did remember. It happened in August 1999. From Poland, where I lived then, we could see only a partial eclipse but still it was something that I took very seriously. I had just turned eighteen and I was allowed a glass of wine with the family meals for the first time. It was the peak of the Polish summer and I was staying at my grandmother's country house.

The place wasn't big but sizeable enough to fit my grandparents, their childless daughter Helena, who lived with them full-time, and me, their only grandson.

My grandparents, by then both pensioners, left their comfortable apartment in Warsaw every year on the 27th of May. The day before, celebrated in Poland as Mother's Day, was also my grandmother's birthday. The birthday which she never celebrated officially. So every year, in the same manner and in accordance with an unstated tradition, my grandmother would invite everyone for a Mother's Day dinner. And at this dinner my father and his sister would approach Granny, wishing her a very happy Mother's Day and then, when leaning over in order to kiss her on her cheek, they would also whisper, "And a very happy birthday". As a response to this my grandmother wouldn't say a word. She only smiled with a bit of disapproval on her face.

The following day, early in the morning, both grandparents would get into their car, packed days in advance, and drive away to their country retreat. Helena would follow them, fulfilling the role more of a companion and a carer rather than the one of a daughter. They would not be back in Warsaw for good until the beginning of September, only occasionally visiting town for a day or two during the summer period, if their doctor's appointments were scheduled for that time.

The house was in an area full of cottages and bungalows used only in the summer months. Only a handful of properties were occupied all year round. In recent years the entire neighbourhood had changed drastically and the surrounding fields were transformed into tennis courts and mini-golf fields. All the roads were covered with asphalt and cars passing by were not accompanied by clouds of sandy dust anymore.

In a way, I think we all felt that it was one of our last summers there. All the other houses in the area already had new owners who either built new, modern dwellings or refurbished the old ones. My grandparents were the last of the original owners who 'colonized' the humble fields, newly divided into building parcels, in the 1950s. And over the following fifty years, my grandparents and their neighbours turned those piles of sand into a magical paradise full of plants, trees and flowers. Soon after they had bought their land, a massive valley only a few hundred yards away, was turned into an artificial lake, which added charm to the area and increased its popularity.

The house itself was very modest, surrounded, however, by the most beautiful plants, for which my grandparents were prepared to pay any price. This little piece of land, so simple and unassuming, they tried to turn into some sort of secret garden, which made them very proud whenever they spoke about it. When in the 1980s my granddad, as an acknowledged economist, gave an interview to the newspaper, he was asked about his hobby. He answered without hesitation, "My country house!" such was his passion for the place.

When they got there for the first time in the season everything was wild and overgrown. Even the house was barely visible. The vines and the roses were climbing the walls. The trees every year were growing more daring than the year before; the plants seemed to be swallowing the house. Only the resilience and determination of my grandparents were tearing the house away from nature and back to us. And as always, it took them only a few days to achieve it. A few days, during which both grandparents, Helena and a local handyman or two were cutting, mowing, removing weeds and fighting back, inch by inch, against nature from morning until evening. Helena, swearing quite loudly, with the help of a hired cleaner, would also tidy the house up: hoovering, wiping the dust away and changing the bed linens. Helena loathed the place. It was difficult to say whether it was because of the house itself or because my grandmother loved it so much, and Helena hated my grandmother. The fact was that they never got on, being so similar to each other.

The summer of 1999 was very different to all the previous ones. Only a few months before, my grandfather was diagnosed with a mild cancer and, considering he was already eighty-one, we all knew he could not live forever. My grandmother knew it too and that year she was even more passionate in planting her roses and azaleas and trimming the hedges which wrapped around the garden. She was so strong-willed and so desperate to live in the moment. Despite being eighty-two herself, she looked like she was mid-sixties and her husband loved that element about her. Every morning he drove to the small town situated two miles away in order to buy a newspaper. Or, I should say, newspapers, as he read many daily papers, and he was as passionate about politics as about his garden. He was always coming back with fresh bread, a new booklet of crosswords: one for himself and one for Helena, and a gift for my grandmother. It could be a woven basket from a local market or a bar of chocolate which they remembered eating from their youth in the 1920s, a bunch of her beloved asparagus, or a new purse. Every day there would be something bought especially for her. And grandmother's reaction was always predictable, just like the existence of Grandfather's gifts – she was genuinely ecstatic. Every day in the same manner and about each and all of the gifts. As Grandfather always knew what mood she was in, all the purchases were capturing exactly something that she was waiting for or what was on her mind.

On that August day, the day of the eclipse, we got up earlier than usual. My grandmother wanted this to be perfect. The rattan chairs were positioned on the lawn and between them there were a few small tables. There were also jugs of juice, biscuits and on the little trays, already melting in the sun, chocolates. For my grandmother it wasn't just the day of the eclipse. It was the day when something extraordinary happened, giving her a break from the obvious routines of the summer. A break from breakfast always served at the same time, a break from eleven o'clock coffee and sweets, from the lunch eaten between one and two in the afternoon, from yet another coffee and cakes at four-thirty and supper served at seven. Every day the entire attention of the household would be focused on those meals and baked cakes and fruit compotes and homemade custard and ice cream and pancakes with fresh fruit. The air was always full of strong smells of home. A real, warm, welcoming Polish home.

Grandmother had a capacity to prepare all the food early in the morning, making running of the entire household look easy. Although she must have been tired, she had never showed it. Later in the day she was always smartly dressed, with her make-up done and a string of corals or some stones around her neck. In the morning she would read her favourite newspaper and in the afternoon a magazine packed with gossip from the lives of the rich and famous. She had so much energy even then, in her eighties. And although my grandparents argued, they loved, respected and admired each other and their fifty-seven years together did not wear it out.

The day before the eclipse, a daily newspaper enclosed special glasses which would protect the eyes from the sun's damage. And on that day we were all proudly wearing them. We could hear the leaves of the fifty-year-old Italian poplar trees and willows moving in the wind, and the barking of our two dogs which were running along the high front fence chasing people cycling on the other side. Even tennis players from the nearby courts, normally heard shouting to each other, were quiet. The sky was clear and the sun was shining. Freshly baked cake was also there, all sticky with its raspberry filling. And Helena was there too, annoyed with the fuss that Grandmother made and ready to provoke an argument. With her dog and her big straw hat, she looked like a cross between Scarlet O'Hara and Blanche DuBois from *A Streetcar Named Desire*.

By then Helena was in her mid-fifties and for my eighteen-year-old-eyes she seemed to be nearly as old as my grandparents.

"Heli! Heli!" My grandmother always used a shortened version of her daughter's name. "Where did you put that china cake stand?" Granny was speaking quite loudly, across the terrace, towards Helena standing on its other side.

"Which one?" By the tone of Helena's voice one knew she was not in a good mood.

"The one with yellow roses on a white background!" Grandmother was impatient.

"Ah, that one? I broke it last week when I was washing the dishes after you had some guests," Helena said with complete nonchalance.

"And what have you done with the pieces?!" Grandmother was showing some signs of desperation.

"I think I binned them...to be honest I don't remember... Anyway it was such an old and ugly thing. No one uses things like that anymore." Helena was pushing it and even she knew it.

"This *ugly* thing, with the entire set for twenty-four people, was given to me by *my* mother on the day of *my* wedding. It was in our family for the last hundred and fifty years and it even bore our family coat of arms. That was the last piece of that set. Everything else was broken in the air raids during the war…" Grandmother was very upset and her voice was shaking.

"Well, it was a stupid thing then to put it out for your guests last week. And anyway, I didn't want that and who else would you pass it on to?" Helena was not taking any prisoners. She wanted an argument and she was going to get it.

"It would be my choice who I would like to pass it to and you wouldn't get it anyway as to get it one has to get married and the last time I checked, you were still a spinster. A fifty-four-year-old spinster!" The last sentence Granny shouted out.

"At least, unlike you, I didn't do everything on the back of a man who I married. In fact, the only reason why you did marry was because you found in dad a 'good enough' match. You never loved him and you never loved me. People like you should never have children…"

An argument was heating up and, as Helena and Grandmother had these sorts of clashes a few times a week, I don't think I was really bothered by its result. I remember that I went back to the lawn on my own. Granddad had by then withdrawn to his crosswords. I poured myself a glass of apple compote and ate a slice of cake. It was warm and I felt happy. The domestic conflicts between those two women, far too similar for either of them to admit, were actually adding to the sense of security and cosiness. Their arguments never went beyond the zone of safety and by then they were simply part of my grandparents' household. I knew very well that by dinner at two o'clock everything would be alright as one of them would apologize and we would all be laughing by the time the dessert was served. We would hear the birds singing and red squirrels jumping between the trees surrounding the open-air veranda, where most of the meals took place.

And sixteen years on, I don't remember seeing the eclipse itself at all. I only have a memory of the day and its smells and the people. I can see them like it was today: my grandparents, Helena, dogs and the house. This world doesn't exist anymore but I still can detect every sense of it and recall its every colour.

"Tom, will you make me a Polish custard after school today?" We could already see the school at the top of the road.

"It depends, Clever Turtle..."

"I will be working really hard at school and I promise to feed my fishes tonight..."

"You have to do it anyway." We were both laughing.

"And I will tidy up my room." She was now giggling, knowing that all her bargaining chips were in fact her daily responsibilities.

"I *will* make you a custard, Clever Turtle. Which flavour would you like?"

"The one that your granny used to make: vanilla...and you could add some of that delicious raspberry jam? It tastes like...home."

The Other Guy

It was a beautiful April day. Saturday. It was also the day of the Grand National, an event very important to a keen horse rider, such as myself. But it was also the day of the Oxford-Cambridge boat race, memorable because for the first time in history women were rowing on the same course and day as men. Cambridge had not won for the last three years and, being a Cambridge alumnus, I was hoping that this time we would give our Oxford 'friends' a lesson they deserved.

My friend Kathy and I went to Putney in order to send both of the teams off at its traditional starting point. The area of Putney Bridge was, as always on that day, very vibrant and full of cheering crowds. The day was warm and sunny but with a strong wind. It felt more like at the Cowes regatta than a river boat race. We went, as every year, to the same pub: the Boathouse. Situated on the other side of Putney Bridge to the place from where the boats launch, it was well known for its bohemian customers.

In the front of the pub there was a band singing in a crazy-twenties-jazz style all the latest pop hits, putting us at ease. Around us there were many Oxford and Cambridge students supporting their teams. Tall, well-built and rather noisy, they brought to this normally quiet part of Putney an unusual sense of life. In their thick, woollen cardigans, skinny jeans and gel-styled hair they looked like people from fashion catalogues. They were also wearing sunglasses by well-known brands and smiled at each other a lot, showing rows of white teeth. Their happy, wealthy faces and good manners, brought an allure of a success and class to this central-London location. It felt as if all the problems of the world didn't exist anymore.

We were having a meal on the terrace of the second floor restaurant, overlooking the river. The afternoon was passing quickly and both Kathy and I were very happy. I was very proud as only a week before my first book had been published. No, not just some ebook, but a good, old-fashioned, paperback. Every morning since I had smelt its pages and touched my name on its front cover. I had been surprised, rather than just happy, that here was my own book. My dream had come true. Kathy was proud too, as after years of renting flats, she has just bought her own first apartment. Full of the joy of the first-time buyer, she couldn't hide her happiness and was in an exquisite mood. She was laughing all the time, sometimes without any obvious reason, and her pashmina, which was moved by the wind, was hitting her face from time-to-time when she was talking. Kathy looked comfortable with herself and the day reminded us both of the time at university when we met, nearly fifteen years before. Since then our friendship had gone from strength to strength. We witnessed each other's successes and failures. First jobs and first redundancies. And, more than it was necessary, broken hearts. Kathy and I knew each other well, understood each other's characters and we never underestimated what we gave to each other.

After lunch we watched the horse race on the pub's screens. Rather tipsy after two jugs of Pimm's, we were shouting and screaming with the others when horses were falling on each of the thirty fences. At the end of the race we jumped and hugged everyone around us, despite the fact that horses we bet on did not even get to the finish. From there we proceeded to the bridge, hoping to wave the women off. The crowds were huge and the helicopters with their cameras were circling above our heads. And then the boats went. We could only see them for a minute or two but this was compensated for by the feeling of excitement usually felt when one witnesses a historically important event. I lifted my head and allowed the wind to mess my hair. In the sky I saw a red balloon filled with helium, which someone, deliberately or not, had sent towards the sun. Prompted by the racing events of the day, I thought how competitive human nature is and this idea was immediately followed by the thought of James.

I had thought about James a lot recently. I had even begun to compare myself to him. I thought of him first thing in the morning when I brushed my teeth (did he also press the brush on his tongue?) and later when I made my morning coffee (did he stir three times left and then twice right like myself?). I carried the thought of him until lunch (would he have a Lebanese sandwich as well or was it too adventurous for him?) and then it recommenced when I was back home from work (was he annoyed as much as I was by women doing their nails on the train?). The last thought of the day was whether he also put earplugs in or if he didn't mind the noises from the streets when he slept.

James would be thirty-seven next week. He always wore

nice, shiny shoes and smelled of the latest fragrance of Dolce & Gabbana. His clothes were perfectly ironed and when you hugged him, or even just touched him, you would be concerned that you might crease them. He was a solicitor by education but a few years back he had decided to switch to an occupation that gave him more time and flexibility and he became a legal consultant. I often wondered what consultants really did but, as he never seemed to have any issue with employment, I assumed that there was a need for the Jameses of this world.

James was five foot eight inches tall and, as a result of his fondness for beer, he grew a little, still not very visible, belly. His hair was fair, a bit ginger. He also had facial hair, which he trimmed daily, paying a lot of attention to this activity. James' partner, Raymond, was American and they had an adopted son together. James lived with his modern family in a small house, in a nice suburb. He liked furnishing his house with shabby chic furniture and he was very proud of his fireplace, which he always decorated for Christmas, in an American manner. James liked climbing and this activity added a certain masculinity to his movements. This, in addition to a deep-grounded confidence, made James a very attractive man, despite the average look and an average intellect. James liked himself. The other men liked James. And I wanted to like James too. But James had had an affair with my partner.

"No, I didn't suspect anything!" I said through the tears to Kathy a few weeks before.

I didn't cry often but I could not stop this time. Patrick and I had been together for many years now and I never expected him to do anything against me. We loved each other and life seemed to make sense together. Much more than that. Until that night when I saw Patrick with James on the street, in central London, I thought we would spend our lives by each other's sides. That was the night when Patrick was supposed to be abroad, with his work. I didn't know anything about James on that night but since then I developed an interest in James and his life. No, not an obsession, just an interest. So now I often imagined that James and I were friends and that, forgetting about the barrier created by his and Patrick's affair, we could go for a drink every now and then.

James was from a good family, like myself. Though British, as a result of his father's position in the Foreign Office he grew up in various European countries. He could also speak a few foreign languages while I sometimes struggled to express myself in my native English. James was sporty, playing rugby and visiting the gym a few times a week. In the gym he didn't exercise much. I saw him from my cross trainer chatting to other men, especially personal trainers. One of them, a black guy, always wearing very tight tops, underlining his muscular chest, seemed to like James more than the others. Whenever James went to the locker room, in order to take a shower, this guy followed. One day I followed James too. I could do all of this unrecognized because I knew James but James did never meet me. I saw him and the other guy going together to the steam room. On the following visits this behaviour turned to a habit and they would always enter and leave the steam room together. I knew what they did to each other in the steam room and I was amazed that they were not scared that they could get caught. The more I watched James, the more I realized that he was very courageous, doing things I would never be daring enough to do.

James provided services to a company in the comfortable suburbs. Its glass three-storey building looked totally out of place in an area filled mostly with big, Tudor-style detached houses. He always got there in his yellow sports car very early in the morning. A time when only lawyers worked while the entire world still slept. He parked his car in the first row, right opposite to the main entrance, on the spacious car park area which wrapped the building from all sides. He locked his car and carried his brown leather briefcase, entering the building with a light walk, just like he was going to a party, not to work.

I never managed to enter the building any further than the reception area. The place had good security and I never felt comfortable in pushing the boundaries, unlike James. I did, however, spend many days at the car park watching the entrance and I knew a lot about James' daily whereabouts.

At precisely one-thirty he left the building, got into his car and drove to a local supermarket. There he always picked a prawn salad and a fresh bread roll. He consciously ate healthily and I liked him for this choice. After lunch, often eaten in his car, he went back to the office, which he never left until six o'clock in the evening. I always thought that lawyers worked longer hours but, considering he was at work from just after six in the morning and worked in the capacity of consultant, twelve hours sounded to me like a pretty busy day already. Every Tuesday and Thursday, after work, James travelled to Parsons Green. He parked his car by a little square opposite to the Aragon Pub and went to a red-brick mansion block around the corner. There he pressed the third button from the top of the long row of buttons. The door opened and he walked into the building. James always stayed there until eight, sometimes eight-thirty. From there he always drove home, though at a higher than his usual speed.

One day I drove to Parsons Green on my own. I stopped the car in front of the same building and watched people coming in and going out of the block. Then I left the car and pressed the same button which now I could see bore the number six. A male voice answered. I didn't prepare myself for it and I walked off without even exchanging a word with the man. I came back on the following evening and worked out that apartment number six was on the second floor on the right hand side from the stairwell. I watched the windows until I saw James and another man embrace each other. Then this other man came to the window and closed the plantation-style shutters, making it impossible for me to see anything else.

I admired James; he managed his time so well while I felt exhausted when I got back from work. I managed to go to the gym only once a week for an hour, while he spent so many of his evenings there when he wasn't in Parsons Green. He also seemed to be exercising daily at home. I could see him doing yoga in his front room every morning. In winter he switched the ceiling light on, while in the summer he opened the window, even when the weather was on the chilly side. He was very bendy and liked to stretch his long upper-body. I could never endure more than five minutes of yoga.

James also drove his son to the football match every Saturday at nine-thirty in the morning. The boy was a good player and James usually came back at one in order to collect him. Sometimes James and Raymond collected him together.

James and Raymond seemed to be a very happy couple. They often laughed when they walked side by side in town or when they shopped in the local deli. Every other Saturday night they went to Soho where they had dinner in a Chinese or Japanese restaurant. Then they went dancing in the 'Village'. James was a good dancer and many men, especially older men, tried to approach him on the dance floor. He smiled to them but always looked towards Raymond who usually sat by the wall and watched James dancing.

One night I followed James to the toilet. When I entered he was just washing his hands. I decided to do exactly the same and went to the nearby washbasin. He looked into the mirror and messed up his hair. And then he looked at me. He smiled at me and he had a beautiful smile. He came closer and put his hand on my back.

"How are you, handsome? Having a good night?" James was obviously drunk but it was the first time I was so close to him and suddenly I felt sick.

"No, I have had an awful day because you had an affair with my partner. Because you were pushing my partner to leave me so that you could take my place in my home and live my life. I hate you and I hope you will die experiencing inhuman pain, the pain I feel every day because of you!"

I thought all this but I didn't say a word to James. I just smiled back and left him behind. I knew I had come too close and I left the club immediately. I turned around the corner and then hid in the little niche between a sex shop and some peep show place. I started vomiting. It was a violent sickness, more violent than I have ever experienced.

I ran home. Literally, I was running across town, pushing people out of my way. I was sweating but I didn't feel tired.

I knew that James, being so fit, wouldn't feel tired either. And I could imagine his wavy hair and his insincere smile during this run. He would be wearing something really smart and even after a five-mile run across London he would look like he had just got dressed – fresh and charming. And I knew I could never be like him because I could never do the things he was doing. I could never wear the clothes he was wearing, I could never smell the way he smelt, I could never exercise as often as he was and I could never find time in my day for all the things he was doing. The things he was doing to himself and to others around him.

My partner could obviously see all this in James. I guess it was easy to be with him – they had no home to run together, no children to look after between them. No washing or ironing to be done. They could just see each other in their nice outfits, in fashionable restaurants in town and in James' house when Raymond and their son were away. They had sex, they ate breakfast together and then they again had sex. Easy, relaxing, without any responsibilities or burdens. But then it was all possible, as it was with James and not me. And James was so good at everything he touched. Successful, ambitious and attractive. He took from life everything he needed and wanted, leaving behind all that drags us down. He had so much. But then there was one thing that I had and James didn't…a conscience.

"Go on! Come on, Oxford!" someone standing behind me in the crowd shouted in my ear.

I looked back towards the screaming man and we smiled at each other. Then I turned my attention to the river and realized that yet another race was about to take place. I also noticed that the red balloon, the same one I saw just a few minutes ago and which reminded me of James, was still in the sky. But now it was pushed by the wind and it was coming down. I decided to follow its track with a sadistic satisfaction and to see it falling. Lower and lower into the river. Eventually I saw this balloon in the Thames, drifting in the strong current of the river. Taken towards the unknown, humiliated and destroyed. It was becoming more and more distant. I tried to follow it, inch by inch, metre by metre, until I couldn't see it anymore. It was too far.

"I think we need another drink," said Kathy walking towards me. I hugged her and she hugged me back.

"Yes, I think we do, sister. You always were a mind reader."

Rush Hour

The train was packed. And I mean *packed*. It looked like you couldn't fit a needle in, not to mention *me*.

I was standing on the platform of West Dulwich station. As every morning I was on my way to work and as every morning I felt intimidated by what was about to happen.

Because *I* wasn't like all the others, like anybody else, really. It hasn't always been like that. When I was young I was just like all the other girls. At least until a certain point. I looked like them until aged sixteen when everything suddenly changed. When *it* had started.

I remember, just like it was yesterday, when I was doing my O levels. Everything seemed to be alright; I was studying on a regular basis and there were no doubts about me doing well. But I did feel scared. I knew that my parents had very high expectations regarding me and my future and I didn't want to disappoint them. I studied every day for many hours. On the request of my father I also had a tutor who made sure that I worked hard enough to get straight As. And I did, but the price was very high.

Food was always an important part of our family life. We all liked eating carefully prepared meals and for that reason we enjoyed daily gatherings around the dinner table. We had a cook, Rosie, an amazing woman from Barbados who was one of those domestic helpers which people had in the old days. Despite not being treated very kindly by my mother, who wanted to be in charge and never allowed Rosie to choose what we were going to eat, Rosie was always smiling and treated every day as a blessing. She went to her church every Sunday, usually attending several services a day: one at eight in the morning, one at ten-thirty and one at twelve. We always knew that we couldn't count on her to make a good Sunday breakfast because Rosie would not be there. My mother tried to pressure her about this issue several times and to make her change her Sunday routines. Rosie, although always nice and resilient, was, however, unbreakable when it came to discussing her Sunday services' attendance. And my mother, though she never did in any other circumstances, had to give in. One day I heard my parents talking about Rosie and I knew that my mother wanted to fire her. But my father, who would never object to my mother about anything, stood up in Rosie's defence and did not allow my mother to get rid of her. I have never known whether it was because my father respected Rosie and her religious beliefs or whether he simply liked her cooking so much. I have always suspected the latter. At least back than it seemed to be the only reason.

Rosie was always there for me. She was kind, sometimes moody but never too busy not to listen to what was happening in my life at the time. My O level worries became obvious to her and she tried to make my life easier by cooking something nice each time my parents were away. During this period I learned to go to the kitchen when I felt tired, anxious or distressed and Rosie would be there, doing her thing and listening.

Rosie was never allowed to eat with my family at the same table. We would have our meals in the dining room but she would eat in the kitchen. I have never understood when she found time to eat herself as she was assisting with our meals and I could not remember her not being in the dining room when we were eating. She would be running to the kitchen in order to bring the first course, then she would take the empty dishes back to the kitchen and would come back with yet another course. Back and forth, without a break.

One day when my parents were away and I was waiting for my meal in the dining room, I decided to go into the kitchen to check how Rosie was doing. She was surprised by my visit at this time of the day and seemed to be intimidated by the fact that I was there. She was just plating the cheese soufflé, which was supposed to be my starter, when I asked her a question. A question which would change our relationship forever,

"Rosie...could I eat in the kitchen tonight?"

Rosie, despite her black complexion, blushed quite visibly. She looked like she misheard or maybe she did not know what to say. After a pause of a few seconds she went to the cupboard where our daily china was kept (there was another set of china in the dining room for Sundays and Christmas) and she took out a starter plate and a main course one, which she carried towards the long wooden table on the other side of the kitchen. She picked only one of each. I felt embarrassed as she clearly did not understand my intentions. I didn't want to be treated like a mistress and her like a servant. I wanted to spend some time with her like two equals. Like friends.

"Rosie," she looked back towards me, "I meant... I would like to eat here with you..."

Rosie was standing there completely lost. She looked upset or offended and it made me feel very uncomfortable.

"I really would like to eat my dinner with you...please... I promise, I will not tell anyone..."

Without another word she went back to the cupboard and picked one plate for herself.

"I am afraid I did not cook enough for two," Rosie said and began to plate my soufflé. "There is only one," she said, looking at me apologetically and then at the soufflé.

"It is not a problem, Rosie, we can share," and I went over to her, took the plate out of her hands and put it in the middle of the table. Then I went to pick up one more starter plate, which I placed next to the chair where I wanted Rosie to sit.

That evening wasn't easy. Although, since I was a little girl, we have always had plenty to talk about, on that night we ate in silence. Nevertheless, I repeated my habit of eating in the kitchen for the entire week of my parents' absence. And each night I had to make a request for her to set the table for two. On the fourth night when I entered the kitchen, I noticed that the table was already covered for two. Rosie looked at me and we smiled at each other.

When my parents got back I had to eat again in the dining room. And I remember that on the first night of their return, I felt that I was betraying Rosie by not eating with her. She must have noticed how torn I was and after the meal she came to me and said:

"Stop worrying. It is normal that there are people who work for other people and that we all have a different place in the world, just like we all have a different place in this household. You cannot torture yourself. They go away often and whenever you would like to, we can eat together in the kitchen. That will be our little secret." And she put her hands on my cheeks, just as if she would like to make me smile.

After that week I ate with Rosie every time there was a chance to do it. And although I don't think my parents would have anything against it, we never told them. We wanted to keep this habit only ours and to maintain its confidential aura. Or at least that was what I wanted.

The exams were coming and I was eating more. Rosie always cooked something extra, only for me. The only time when I felt good and relaxed was when I had a plate full of warm food in front of me. And the comfort the food brought became addictive. I wanted to feel good all the time and I wanted the pressure to go. A few weeks later Rosie noticed that there was something wrong with me. That I was eating more than it was necessary, more than was healthy. Once she approached this subject with her simple honesty,

"Are you worried about something, darling? I see you coming down here a few times a day. And I like your company, but you cannot eat that much. You are young and young girls should not be too plump. You are pretty and you do sports but recently you put on weight. More than...is right for you..."

Whilst she was talking I looked into her face but by the last sentence I was staring at the floor. Embarrassed and confused I began to cry. Rosie came to me and gave me a big hug. I hugged her back but I felt hurt. Only later, I understood that she meant well. That she was right.

After my O levels the A level exams came and the entire routine was on again. I was eating with my family, then I would go to the fridge and pick various snacks from there until I realized that it was too visible and I began to hide things in my room. I had several hiding places: one under my bed, another in the wardrobe and one more behind the books on the bookcases. I hid sweets, chocolates and sometimes even sandwiches, which I would make for myself when everyone, including Rosie, was already sleeping.

The food brought me a sense of security which I never had before. My home wasn't very warm. In fact the only person who made this place a home was Rosie. My father was very distant and isolated. Today he would probably be diagnosed with some form of Asperger's syndrome but back then, in the seventies, no one thought that his behaviour was not 'normal'. He struggled socially and I could never quite understand how he could do his job. As a foreign affairs newspaper correspondent he was often travelling and he must have felt very intimidated by all the people he met during those journeys. He wasn't a bad person. But he was an absent person. Someone you would not notice when he was there and...who you would never miss when he was away.

My mother was different. Socially ambitious and intelligent, sometimes I used to think that my dad's career was her success. She was always travelling with him and entertaining many people who could be important for my father's development and his employment prospects. She was a good woman, although very strict and cold. And she wasn't able to show me her love because, just like her mother and grandmother, my mother did not have a maternal instinct. She didn't mean to be like this. The instinct was not in her and she couldn't help it. This made her a distant parent, just like my father was. Because both of them had their parental instincts disabled, each in their own way.

My mother was, however, much more present as a lady of the house. She was the one furnishing the house, making it always look presentable and attractive. And for many other people, the outsiders as I used to call them, due to my mother's hosting skills, our house was the synonym to a perfect home. Not many people knew though how cold and lonely those warm spaces could be with parents like mine.

After my A levels I went to university. That was the beginning of me the way I am now. I was free and I did not have to obey any of the rules of my mother. I shared the house with many other, equally lost, young students. However, they seemed to find peace in the company of each other. They partied together, cooked together, slept together. I was on my own. And my only rescue was my food. In those days I was eating all the time. The first thing I did when I woke up was to run into the kitchen in order to get a plate full of biscuits. From that moment every hour, every half hour I would go the kitchen to prepare something to eat. Soon even my housemates noticed this and they started calling me a vacuum cleaner, which then transformed into a hoover and this in turn was cut short to Huv. This became my nickname for the entire period of my higher education.

Initially this mild form of bullying, accompanied by everything else that happened at university, bothered me a lot. But soon I learnt to ignore it. The comfort which my food gave me was worth all sorts of sacrifice. When I graduated I was already big. Not as big as now but my size was already significant enough that I was forced to have my graduation robe tailored. But it wasn't all that bad. I graduated with distinction and I was headhunted by a big City firm, even before passing my final exams. The way I am now I became soon after I married Heino.

It was after I came back to London from the funeral of Rosie. She hadn't been well for all my university years and I was grateful to my parents that they did not fire her as soon as she became ill. But the years when I was away brought – somehow – my parents and Rosie closer. Maybe my parents felt left on their own after I moved out or maybe they simply realized what Rosie had done for them for over twenty-five years when she worked for them, making their house a home. During my last visits from university their relationship seemed to have gone through a massive transformation. They began to treat her like a member of the family. She was even eating her meals with them, in the dining room. Whether it was because they realized that they had nothing, or rather nobody else, left in their lives or because my mother eventually accepted the fact that my father loved Rosie and had had an affair with her for the many years Rosie spent with them, I will never know. Because they did have an affair. I discovered it a few weeks before my A levels when I found a letter from my dad in the kitchen. The letter was addressed to Rosie and, although I shouldn't have, I read it. The tone of this correspondence was sufficient to understand what was going on between those two. However, even if the tone had been different, the words themselves provided an expressed evidence of what was between them.

Despite the fact that the affair hurt my mother, I was happy about this discovery. And it wasn't because I did not feel much for my mother but because I cared about Rosie so much and this made her a member of my family. Or at least she became a member of my family to me.

Only many years later did I understand how this situation must have hurt my mother. It could have provided an explanation to many of her behaviours. Maybe that is why she was always on edge: chasing my father, checking where he was, what he was doing and enquiring who he was talking to every time he left the room. And maybe that was why she wanted to fire Rosie years before.

But what happened next went far beyond what I could ever expect from my mother. When Rosie was dying, my mother looked after her. And she did it like she would do for a member of her family, not domestic help. My mother was patiently feeding Rosie, washing her and reading her daily newspapers. She was even crying during Rosie's funeral. At the same time my dad did not show any sadness. He was as apathetic as he has always been. The funeral changed my views about my mother despite the fact that it had no impact on our future relationship.

I came back to London on the day after the funeral. I wasn't very upset – I had lost Rosie many years before, when I went to university. And I learnt to cope with my losses, in my own usual way. By eating.

Coming to London also meant quite a painful change in the dynamics of my life. It always did take me some time to settle in in new places and I experienced this each time I came back to university from my parents' house. At university, life was thriving. There, in my parents' house, there was no life. London was far more vibrant and hectic than anything else I had a taste of before, and it took much longer to adjust to this final move than I would have wanted.

I met Heino on the streets of Islington, where I lived back then. One day I turned from Northampton Square towards St

Johns Street and I literally bumped into a man. He collapsed, dropping a box of papers he was carrying. I apologized but he invited me for a drink. His name was Heino and he was Dutch. As I was on my way to meet my old friend, I couldn't accept the invitation but we exchanged phone numbers and promised to meet soon.

I didn't think that someone like Heino would genuinely like to go for a drink with me. I thought he only suggested this out of courtesy, to show some kindness to a fat woman in her mid-thirties who nearly caused him an injury. I thought that because my personal life had never been good. Or I should say I have never had any personal life.

I had been on several dates and I rapidly realized that with every extra pound of my flesh I took one step down in terms of the type of man I could date. At first those men were lawyers, like me. Proper, stiff, a bit boring, but successful, though average-looking. Soon I was out of the league of those so I turned to accountants. Some of them were obese, like myself. But later even those most average looking and moderately exciting would not be interested in a girlfriend who struggled to fit into a chair in the restaurant and would eat two main courses during an evening date. Eventually, I went for men of trade, as my mother used to call them. Many of them were well built and quite successful financially. Some were even more successful than many of the accountants I had dated before, and all of them were definitely much more interesting and exciting than the lawyers. To them I was a different type of attraction. Although I was in a size way above what could be defined as broadly acceptable, I had something they found very impressive. That was my background and my job. So they treated me like a perverse trophy, showing to their friends that they managed to conquer an upper-class woman who doesn't need their money. After those experiences I did not hope for anyone different to ever enter my life.

But three days after our crash on the street Heino called me and invited me for dinner. I could not believe my luck. We talked all the time, without hardly any breaks, looking into each other's eyes. He didn't even blink when I ordered two desserts and waited patiently for me to finish. Heino was different to the other men I dated before. He was thin and quiet. Good-looking in a romantic way, with an aura of secretiveness. He was not interested in me being fat or slim, he did not show any interest in my job or background. Heino was interested in me, the person I was under nearly two hundred and fifty pounds of flesh.

We started seeing each other a few times a week, then daily, until we decided to move in together.

Initially all was going really well. We were laughing at the same things and enjoying all, even the most simple of activities. But gradually things became more difficult. Heino had a very short temper and occasionally, when in anger, he could explode. When he was in distress he was also verbally aggressive. On the following day after any such incident he would always apologize and I, consequently, did not take much notice of his anger. After all, the beginning of every relationship, when people start living together and clash, is a challenging time for everyone involved. It was natural, I thought, that being on our own for so many years, both Heino and myself, developed certain habits and routines which were not easy to accommodate for either party. After any such clash Heino would retire to bed falling asleep almost immediately afterwards. I couldn't sleep so I would walk downstairs to the kitchen and eat. But this time it was a different eating. At my parents' home, at university or later during my adult life I was eating more because it was giving me pleasure and comfort. I did care what I ate and I always ate meals which were tasty, carefully prepared; only the portions I would make for myself increased in size as time went by. With Heino it was different. I was eating just for the sake of it. It was not in search of pleasure and safety anymore. Eating became my hobby, a type of replacement activity which was compensating for everything I did not have in my life. I started to eat things straight out of the fridge, the way they were, so that the only time when various types of food were mixing with each other was in my mouth or rather stomach. Raw vegetables, cold frankfurters, coleslaw salads eaten from the pack and chocolates, plenty of chocolates. Sometimes in one hand I had a Cornish pasty and in the other a Mars bar. At the same time, eating simultaneously.

I knew it wasn't right and I knew that my relationship with Heino had something to do with this change in my habits. But because I had eaten so much for many years, even before I met Heino, I didn't think that he and my 'new' eating could be linked directly. We had a good time too, I thought, when Heino was not angry or depressed. As after a period of anger, depression followed. He would often be sitting in the attic room, which he used as his study, and would not speak to me for hours, or days if it was a weekend. Initially I thought he needed some quiet time on his own but then I understood that he had a problem.

After a medical consultation he was diagnosed with depression and a psychologist who made Heino do various tests confirmed that he had bipolar disorder. That explained the long weeks of sadness but also the days when he was very active and believed that he could achieve all his life goals or even more. On those good days he would take me for dinner or to the cinema and I felt like a princess with a knight on a white horse by my side. Now, after the diagnosis, I realized that even those good moments might have been the result of the illness, not his feelings towards me. And all the time when we dealt with Heino's diagnosis and therapy, I ate. Despite going to a psychiatrist with Heino, it did not occur to me that I had a problem too and that they might have helped me, just like they tried to help Heino. Because I was so much focused on Heino's needs, I simply did not think that I should ask for some help as well. My eating didn't harm anybody and it did not make anyone unhappy or miserable. And I did like my food, despite the fact that it changed me to the size of the woman I was now.

A month after diagnosis Heino proposed. Initially I was hesitant. After being brought up in my parents' home, I didn't know whether I ever wanted to have a proper family. Even the type of family without any children, containing only a husband and wife; two people who were supposed to look after each other and to be there for the other party in need. Then I thought about the good times we had had and about the fact that I did love Heino. I also knew it could be my last and only chance to be with someone for good. I said yes.

After our wedding, for several months, our life together was pleasant. Heino's condition was stabilizing and I didn't feel on edge with him anymore, expecting his depression to come back anytime. Six months into our marriage I felt that my life was beautiful. I felt genuinely happy and I wanted to spend my entire life with Heino. I also thought, for the first time, about going on a diet or some sort of eating habits therapy.

But then Heino's illness came back. And I became his carer. I thought that already working long hours, I did not have time to look after myself and my diet, because I had to look after Heino. Again. Or maybe there would be enough time but I liked the comfort of eating too much. The food was giving me the only sense of security and belonging I had ever had.

The train was approaching. I moved towards the place on the platform where the door of the train should be positioned when the train stopped. The other people gathered there too and I felt their eyes on me. Because people were staring at me wherever I went. I couldn't care less about any of this anymore and I did not care then. In forty-five minutes I would get to work. I will sit at my desk comfortably and for the next eleven hours, my only movements will be a walk to the work canteen where everyone knows me and my appearance will not surprise anybody. And anyway, I was too senior to cause any comments, or at least any comments to my face. The ones behind my back were not my concern.

Next to me was a lady who looked just like Rosie. Although her appearance looked nothing like Rosie's, her smile and mannerisms were just like hers and it made her, in my eyes, someone so similar to my parents' old cook. I smiled back at her. And I thought about Rosie and about the last dessert she served me. It was based on an amazing Italian recipe which she'd learned from her previous mistress, who had come to England from Florence. The delicate thin *savoiardi* biscuits crushed into a martini glass. They must have been soaked before in some sort of coffee, maybe espresso, liqueur. This in turn was covered in a sweet and fluffy mascarpone and cream mix, on the top of which there was a generous spread of grated dark chocolate. I remember how Rosie smiled when she saw me on the first day of that visit to my parents, when she was still alive and well. And I remember, even more vividly, the flavour of this pudding. Then I thought about Heino being on his own at home and about yet another evening during which we would be avoiding each other in the house, each in their own room, distant and lonely. I felt hungry. I couldn't wait to get to work, to go to the canteen and to order a big, fruity bowl of porridge. And then I could have a bagel with salmon. Even the thought of this treat calmed me down and braced me for what was about to come.

I started to squeeze myself into the crowd, just like everyone else, making sure I would get into the approaching carriage. The train was already full of people but, like every day, I knew I had to get into the seven-twenty-four train to be able to have my breakfast at work before my first conference call.

The train stopped. I was pushed by a flood of people attempting to get in. I decided to make use of my body and push even harder, making sure that I would be one of those few lucky early-morning-passengers who would find a space on this train. I already had my right foot on the carriage's floor but the people inside did not want to move any further.

"Could you move to the far end of the carriage, please?" I shouted across the crowd my daily request. "There is still plenty of space there."

"Not when she gets on," I heard a man behind me whispering to the person next to him. I did not turn. This sort of comment was a part of my daily life. And I had a much higher stake on the table here.

I pushed in some more so that the balance of my body was on the train, though my bottom, or the majority of it, was still sticking out. I kept pushing. I had to have time for that porridge. And the bagel. I heard the signal announcing the door being closed. I pushed in one more time, with the full strength of my body so that in the last minute my entire shape got squeezed in, just in time to avoid it being hit by the shutting door. I took a deep breath. I felt a sense of achievement. I would have enough time for breakfast. Life wasn't that bad after all.

Pure Happiness

It was my last day in London and I felt ecstatic. I was walking along Regent Street and looked confidently into the faces of the crowds passing me by. They all came here to see the sights and to admire, while I was running away. Exhausted and haunted like a wounded animal.

The previous night I had dinner with Luigi and Carlo, my two Italian friends. The evening was funny, easy and, as always, filled with Italian food. We were all laughing and joking, understanding that it may take us a while to see each other again. We'd had evenings like this every week for the last three years, since the day we met. Although it was sad to lose them and their company, this didn't dampen my mood. I had known for a while by then that it was time for a change and my recent inheritance made it all the more possible.

Only four months ago I was about to leave the house for work when I received a letter. I was working shifts, just like most retail employees in London and on that day I was starting at eleven-thirty. Although I knew that if I didn't leave soon, I would be late, I decided to submit myself to yet another explosion of bad temper from my boss, and I opened the letter immediately. Something in me was telling me to do it there and then. And its contents did not disappoint me.

It was a letter from a solicitor. I was informed that an old aunt of mine from Paris, a relative I hadn't seen for the last ten years or so, had passed away and in her will she left me an apartment. Aunt Amélie was an older sister of my grandmother or, to be correct, her half-sister. They shared a father but not their mothers. To be exact, Aunt Amélie's mother was left for the mother of my grandmother, my grandmother being a love child. Aunt Amélie did not get on with my grandmother and the grudge had only widened and deepened over the years. I don't think that there was anything in them, personally or characteristically, that could justify the lack of fondness and the hostility they held towards each other. It was the conduct of their father that chased them and disconnected them for their entire lives. Years later, my mother began a correspondence with Aunt Amélie, keeping this strictly secret from her own mother. As a result she met Aunt Amélie once or twice a year, travelling especially to Paris for that purpose. Since my mother passed away, my link to this part of the family seemed to be broken forever. To be honest, I was sure that Aunt Amélie must have died years before.

Aunt Amélie never had her own family but had achieved something that in many ways we could call success. For years she had worked as a secretary and was the right hand to a chairman of a big international organization and somehow she managed to accumulate a small personal fortune. She had several flats in the attractive parts of Paris, which she bought in the sixties and seventies, when prices were still for the pocket of an average earner. Sometimes I thought that that was the reason why she did not have her own family – she was too busy building her own, hard-earned wealth. According to the letter, despite not seeing each other for so many years and not cultivating any family connections, Aunt Amélie did not forget about her only living relative – me. The letter stated that I had been left one of her apartments in Paris. Only later I discovered that it was a small studio flat in the sixteenth arrondissement. For a second I wondered what happened to all the rest she possessed but then the joy of having an apartment in Paris, no matter how small, overtook everything else. And on the day I received the letter I did not go to work.

I was overwhelmed with the sudden change of my circumstances: from a penniless graduate, working part-time in a boutique in Brompton Road, to a mortgage-free property owner at the age of twenty-five. For years, since my mother passed away and I moved to London, I had struggled financially. With no help and the lack of any assets I was studying and working at the same time. Sometimes it meant having no days off for weeks.

My work wasn't great fun. I managed to get a relatively well-paid job in a fancy shop in Brompton Road thanks to my looks. From the very beginning Tatiana, the fifty-something-year-old Russian owner of the establishment, decided that I looked appropriate to work for her. She wanted to have some handsome men in the shop and I fitted the requirements. She was a divorcee of one of the many Russian millionaires who settled in London since Putin had come to power and who abandoned her for a younger woman soon after the move. As soon as they arrived in London, according to Tatiana, 'the bastard' met a nineteen-year-old girl and left Tatiana, paying her off with the boutique and a few other properties across Knightsbridge. Even Tatiana couldn't quite say how her ex made his fortune but she was willing to accept any of his actions, as long as she was not short of cash.

Initially I was working at Tatiana's for three days a week – including the weekends – and sometimes it wasn't easy. The shop was very busy, occasionally closing down for private shopping sessions of various well-off and extremely rude compatriot-friends of our owner. They spent dozens of thousands of pounds on clothes they never had a chance to wear and often came back the following week for yet more clothes. But my work colleagues – Luigi and Carlo – became my best friends and soon going to work was bearable only because of them. With Luigi and Carlo work could be funny and light-hearted, and even the awful manners of our customers could be softened by their small and innocent jokes. We worked together and socialized together. We even spent the Christmas and Easter holidays in one of our places, sharing everything we had. Three foreigners lost in an alien city. Far away from home and lonely, we became a home to each other.

I moved to London three years before in order to pursue my education. Having no one to care for or to be cared by, I had the freedom to choose my future. My head was full of grand ideas of what I would do and could do and I had no doubts that my success was just around the corner. But with time passing, my life was slowly crushing my dreams. While completing my course, the recession came and London was no longer as friendly as it used to be. There were no jobs and no one wanted to hire a foreign employee in the City at a time when so many British young professionals were unemployed. So my retail job, initially only a support for my education plans, suddenly, with the completion of the course became my full-time career with no prospects for anything interesting. I did send many CVs and covering letters but the response was always negative. Even a consultation with the specialist recruiters did not help. They told me that my hopes for a professional career, in the circumstances where so many companies were winding up, were minimal and that I should maybe think of something more appropriate. This possibly meant cleaning or becoming a plumber – a typical occupation of my Polish compatriots. After a conversation with Tatiana, she took pity on me and offered me more hours in the shop. The job was paid well enough to survive but not enough to make any progress with life. All other jobs that I could have undertaken and which got a welcoming response from employers were in administration, with the salaries exceeding minimum wage only very slightly. My pay at Tatiana's shop was much more advantageous than those.

Tatiana wasn't a pleasant employer. She would help you if you needed it but only if the entire world knew that she did and if you really begged her. In all other circumstances she would be hell. She would shout at us in front of the customers, boss everyone around and make us to do things which gave her a perverse satisfaction. She always wanted to crush our spirits and make sure we would never leave, or at least not as long as she needed us. As a result I was working long hours in her shop and in the evenings I would be sending out other job applications. Month after month, endlessly.

I lived in a house in Fulham. In the rougher part of Fulham, I should say. My landlord, Rutheford, was a forty-something Anglo-American guy. He had lived in London for his entire life, in the same house, which previously belonged to his parents. He was a bachelor and although he has been outspoken in his rather racist and homophobic views,

I always thought that his dream was to settle with a middle-aged black guy. Rutheford made some discreet advances and ambiguous comments towards me many times but because they contrasted sharply with his other opinions, I could pretend that I did not understand what he meant. I only made sure that the door to my room was always properly shut before I went to bed every night. Just in case. Apart from being a bit slimy, Rutheford was a decent guy and a few times when I couldn't pay my rent on time, he would patiently wait. Even if he hoped for any sort of reward in exchange, he never crossed the line and we lived relatively amicably under one roof for the entire period of my London life.

With the time passing my situation became increasingly uncertain. I was educated and young but I could not live all my life working in the shop and renting a room at Rutheford's. Something that was interesting and exciting for a student became a painful and rather challenging existence for an adult man.

The constant humiliation at work and lack of luck with any other jobs brought me closer to Luigi and Carlo. They were both older and with a past of their own but, despite the differences, we had a lot in common and our friendship blossomed. Carlo was in his mid-thirties while Luigi in his early forties and they both, initially, seemed to be very mature. But the more I get to know them, the more I realized that the most mature person amongst the three of us was myself. The first time we all went out was nearly two years before. It was supposed to be just for a drink. We ended up being out for the entire night, changing bars and pubs during the course of the evening and laughing lots. I do not remember a time when they did not make me laugh. They had a fantastic,

Italian approach towards life. They took life just the way it was, without any unnecessary complications, ignoring everything that was against them, and being grateful for all the good that crossed their paths.

Carlo was well educated and he came to London from Milan to broaden his horizons and for success, like I had. But he had failed and was too embarrassed to go back home. His family had very high expectations of him and he resented going back, knowing that they would be watching him very carefully and that he would feel their breath on his neck all the time. In London he was free, at least, and could tell them anything about his life. And no matter what nonsense he made up, so far, they seemed to be buying it.

With Luigi the situation was different. He was from a very poor family from Calabria. He had lived in Palermo for many years where he was married and had two daughters, who he adored. But many years into the relationship, as a result of his affairs, he got divorced and after his wife kept all they had, he struggled to survive in Italy on his own. Coming to London meant a massive change for him. His jobs, as he was also working as a taxi driver, allowed him not only to send sufficient money home for his daughters but also to live a much better life than he could ever have had if he stayed in Sicily. What was for Carlo and me a degradation was for Luigi a big step up, and the only thing that sometimes showed the differences between us three was the discrepancy regarding our opinions on this.

There was one thing Carlo and Luigi had in common. They were both extremely good-looking, though in a very different way. Carlo was blonde with a tanned complexion, a very unique combination seen sometimes in northern Italy.

Luigi was dark and, with his olive skin and penetrating big black eyes, could pass for an Arab. Very soon after I started to work for Tatiana I understood that she expected her staff to sleep with her. Both Carlo and Luigi did, although that was the only subject I would never mention with them. Being so fond of them I somehow found it dirty, disgusting and degrading. It clashed with everything I felt towards them as my friends and, at the time, as my only family. Despite the lack of conversation about them and Tatiana, they must have realized what my opinion was about this conduct and when initially she was making passes at me, they managed to convince her that I was gay. I was very grateful for their support and their lie about my sexuality spared me many difficulties with my employer.

Luigi and Carlo, being so different but sharing the same Italian passion for life, merged as friends quite naturally, if not organically. In a typical Catholic dichotomy they could sleep with our boss during the week but on Sunday they would be the first at the morning mass in the Italian church in Farrington, praying with vigour and devotion quite easily. They took me to their church several times and it was very warming to see them feeling so at home on this little piece of Italian soil in London. Because both Luigi and Carlo disliked Britain and the British. They couldn't understand the ugliness and busyness of London's day-to-day life and couldn't comprehend the lack of open-mindedness amongst the British towards other nationalities living around them. But they could not see that by having these views, they actually fitted perfectly well into British society where every group, whether social, religious or ethnic, felt justifiably superior to all the other groups. And here there were two Italians who could not understand why the entire population didn't want to be and act like Italians.

The best part of our lives together were Christmas Day and Easter Sunday – the only two days in the year which we all had off at the same time as the shop was closed. We would start the day by going to their Italian church after which we would gather at Luigi's little flat in Surbiton – out of the three of us he was the only one owning a property here – where we would all cook various meals from the cuisines of our homelands. They would constantly argue between themselves about the way in which the food should be cooked, clashing between the recipes of northern and southern Italy. After hours of preparations we would sit in the little sitting room, eat, chat and listen to good music, mostly jazz. It would be like home and we all understood the importance of our place in each others lives and the meaning of our time together. We were uprooted foreigners living in hostile land with no real family or homes. Therefore, we became home to each other, understanding at the same time that this was only temporary, as our lives would take different directions one day. We were just like boys in boarding school who spend ten or so of the most important years of their childhood and adolescence under the same roof, often never seeing each other again in adult life. All three of us knew it, but what Luigi and Carlo didn't know was that I was very scared of losing them as they were all I had.

When Aunt Amélie died and I inherited my flat in Paris, I called both of them immediately in order to share the news. I was ecstatic as I thought that from that moment our lives would be easier. Both of them, however, immediately asked me when I was going to leave. I felt hurt, deeply hurt. The conversation continued on that night at a dinner we had together in a little Italian restaurant in Putney.

"Guys, don't you understand? It is going to be a change for all of us. We can sell it and invest into a business or we can travel...or simply have a more exciting life here!" I was nearly shouting in my happiness.

"Don't be ridiculous!" Luigi said. "You have to spend your money for your own needs. It is not ours – it is yours and you deserve it!"

"But we are like a family, I don't want to have a good life and leave you to...to this..."

"I am going to lose it with this idiot!" Carlo chipped in in his typical manner. "Don't you understand that you are different? You are far too intelligent to be here and you have to pursue what you always hoped for in life. This is a perfect opportunity for you, not for us. Grow up – we are not a family! We are friends and tomorrow you will have new friends, wherever you decide to go... And we will do the same – won't we, Luigi?"

"Of course we will. Or we find ourselves girlfriends and will not give a fuck about you!" Luigi added.

I left the restaurant in a foul mood. They clearly did not comprehend what they meant to me and how prominent a position in my life their friendship had. Only later I understood what they had tried to do and tell me. A few days after our meal in Putney, we had a dinner again. It was just like nothing had happened before and we never went back to the conversation. However, we did talk about what I could do with the money and Carlo came up with an idea of me doing a PhD, something I have always wanted to do. He even found some courses in Florence which were run in English during the first year and then in Italian during the following two. By the second year of the course students were supposed to be fluent enough in Italian to be able to carry on the course in that language. That could be a perfect opportunity for me as I had always liked travelling and learning new languages. It also could lead to a future career as a lecturer or researcher and I felt moved with the extent to which Carlo understood me and how much he tried to help me.

Now, several months later, I was a prospective PhD student on my last day in town. I had already emptied my room and said goodbye to Rutheford, who was crying. I had my last dinner with Carlo and Luigi the night before. We all played it cool and pretended that nothing different was happening, that the world was not going to change for us in the slightest. We all treated the entire situation like a business arrangement, with a distant professionalism, although since I had received my inheritance I could always count on their help and advice. With the application process Carlo was irreplaceable and Luigi transported all my possessions to his apartment where he allowed me to leave them, only gradually moving them with me, wherever I would end up. The latter made me especially happy as it meant that we would still have a link between us.

After our last dinner we gave each other a hug and only during this hug I had a chance to witness how much I meant to them. Those two tough Italians were crying and could not stop hugging me. On that night we all knew – though I was the last one to come to terms with it – that we were like ships that pass in the night. We gave each other warmth and friendship and support but our time to separate had come. All three of us accepted it, despite the fact that it hurt.

I could not stop thinking of them and about everything they meant to me. But then I also could not stop thinking how it would be in Italy – with me doing my course, me learning Italian, me living the life that Carlo and Luigi showed me. I could not wait for all of what was yet to come and instead of being sad, I felt excited.

I looked at a long handwritten list of things I wanted to buy for my journey – some clothes, English books, accessories (so important in Italy) – and then I thought that I would buy something for Carlo and Luigi. Anything, just to show them how much I appreciated their presence...and their legacy. *"Life doesn't tolerate any limbos: when something ends, something else, very often much better, immediately starts"* – I remembered the last sentence that Luigi had said the night before. Yes, my friends, I thought, but those new, beautiful things began only because of those things that ended.

Vicious Little Bitch

Anna was running through the lobby of the university hall. She didn't know what had just happened but she felt she couldn't take it. She couldn't see any of those people again. She had to leave.

Anna had always been her parents' pride. Being born nearly eleven years after her older sibling, she brought a fresh change to the deteriorating marriage of her parents and allowed them to experience parenthood the way they never had before. At the time of the birth of her two older brothers, Anna's parents were too busy working, building their careers and their assets. Only with Anna was this all already in place and they could experience everything that they missed with Josh and Thomas.

A year after Anna was born her parents bought their seven-bedroom house near Chipping Norton, and were gradually adding elements that would shape its later splendour. The barn was built and the heated swimming pool, and the two bedroom tree house, and the guest-turned-nanny cottage. All situated on nearly twelve acres of an estate with woodlands and evergreen lawns. Everything was provided for Anna, who by the age of five was the only one out of three children still living with her parents. With her brothers at boarding school and university respectively, she received her parents' entire and undivided attention. Soon after Josh and Thomas moved out, Anna began to use their rooms and her numerous toys and clothes could be found in all three bedrooms. As every bedroom had an en suite, she also used their bathrooms and had a habit of having a morning shower in Josh's bathroom and the evening bath in her own.

Josh and Thomas had grown up in a traditional semi-detached house in Wimbledon and while their parents were working long hours, their main carer was their paternal grandmother. As a result, both boys did not really establish a strong bond with their parents and their sudden wealth was something they have never learnt to use. They struggled in boarding schools, being so different to most of the boys, as their childhood experiences were not comparable to the ones of their colleagues and it was impossible to bridge this gap sufficiently quickly. Their best friends were usually boys who were admitted to the school on the basis of scholarships and who, just like Josh and Thomas, did not understand their rich fellow pupils.

With Anna things were very different. Adored by her parents, not knowing her brothers very well, she was brought up like only children often are: precious, isolated, spoiled and lonely. No expense was spared to make her happy and she had everything she merely thought of or she had ever mentioned. Her parents thought about sending her to boarding school but they decided against it. They did not want to part from her, such a close connection they had. The decision to keep her at home longer only deepened the grudge between Josh and Thomas and their parents and did not help in their relationship with Anna. Anna always felt that her brothers did not like her but she was used to jealousy and separation from others and it did not bother her. She had her parents and they had the money. She could have everything she wanted.

Anna went to a local primary school. But it was not a typical school – not only was it a public school but it gathered all the children of the elite who owned houses similar to the one of her parents. Amongst her school friends were the children of famous politicians, actors and the youngest descendants of the deposed Yugoslavian royal family with their funny, unpronounceable surname. All those people became Anna's friends and through those friendships Anna's parents' social position grew respectively too. Thanks to Anna, her parents began to receive invitations to the houses they never thought of visiting before.

Due to the family money Anna could afford to do anything with her life and future, and as a result of the friendships she made at schools, she could get the help or advice from many people of importance. The power that her position gave her began to influence the way she was with other people less fortunate than her. She started being rude to those who could not do anything for her or who in any way depended on her family. At first she was trying this 'different approach' with people working for her parents and when they did not complain about her harsh tone of voice, Anna adopted this way of speaking as her own. Her parents did not notice any difference in her. In their eyes she was always the most kind, talented, pretty and hard working person they have ever came across. The truth was that by fitting in so easily with the cream of society Anna impressed them and they felt proud that, unlike themselves, their daughter really belonged there.

Both in primary school and the even more expensive secondary school, Anna thrived. She wasn't pretty but always well dressed and she got very good grades. She was always amongst the very popular girls because Anna knew how to make others like her. She always said the 'right' thing to the right people. She could be kind and pleasant and, when no one knew, manipulative. Anna would always get what she wanted and her group of friends was accustomed to accommodating that. They realized very quickly that if they were not with her, she would consider them to be against her. And Anna was a very powerful enemy to have. Because of her skill of manipulation and a sharp tongue Anna knew not only how to make other pupils do what she wanted but she also knew how to involve the teachers in her games.

After completing school Anna went to St Andrews University in Scotland. The choice of the school was obvious to her parents and they fully approved. That was the place where the future Queen of England, known then as Kate Middleton, met her husband and it had become a Mecca ever since for every aspirational family in Britain with daughters of the eligible age. Although there were no more princes left to marry, there were descendants of other sufficiently important families present. Besides, even association with such high circles by becoming a member of the same alumni society was already pleasant enough to Anna. She studied history and, although the subject did not interest her in the slightest, the atmosphere of the school did not disappoint her. She was again popular but this time amongst a different group of people. She only had two girlfriends, surprisingly similar to her both in look and character, but one could find many more boys or rather young men in her circle. In order to be more visible to the opposite gender, she also changed her sense of fashion and began a diet which quickly made her a skinny, fragile and Holly Golightly-like young woman.

At university Anna also realized that she would like to do something more meaningful with her career and by the second year she had already decided to become a solicitor. Anna's parents were surprised by this choice, thinking until then that all Anna wanted was to marry well. They were, obviously, willing to pay for whatever she chose to do in future and they have decided that after the completion of the course Anna would start the Graduate Diploma in Law. That would allow her to get a law degree within a year, after which she would be able to undertake a year-long professional course for solicitors. All those courses would take place in London. Anna's father already began to call his various influential friends and business partners in order to find her valuable work experience. Not that Anna needed any help. She was intriguing against other, prettier, girls, and ignored all those who got to the university on a scholarship, university loan or on the mercy of some distant relatives. She had also had two relationships with the young men of sufficient standing, which ended up with them being publicly humiliated by her, so much so that one changed university and the other left the idea of graduating for good. However, despite her lack of any moral values or good character, no one could refuse Anna her brightness. She always got the highest possible grades, not because teachers liked her or were scared of her but because she studied hard and had great potential. Therefore Anna's life was full of paradoxes – she was attractive but not pretty, she was liked despite the fact that most people found her vicious, and she was very clever, although she studied only for 'competing' and 'winning', not because she wanted to gain any real knowledge. And in all this dichotomy Anna was on the winning side, making her many negative traits her assets and by masking well those which she couldn't transform.

At the end of her time in St Andrews Anna got engaged to Tristan. Her fiancé wasn't what everyone, including her parents, had expected. He was from a good family in the sense that his father was a local GP but was far away from the circles in which Anna usually functioned. Tristan was, however, a top student and his lecturers said that he had a great future in front of him. To Anna the choice of Tristan was very conscious. She dropped the idea of falling madly in love and she planned to live her life with someone who would be grateful for 'having' her and would treat her in a way that everyone else did so far. Tristan's rather geeky looks helped her too. Standing next to him made her only more visible, as his ugliness underlined her good features, making out of her something she had never really been – a beautiful woman. Her social circle was disappointed with the choice of Tristan as her future husband but Anna had an explanation to defend him ready. After all, he did belong to their 'chosen' group by being with her (therefore being an 'equal') and, due to his exceptional intelligence, she could foresee for him a bright career. What she did not say out loud, but what she hoped for, was that she could play a leading role in this career, in case hers did not go so well.

When Anna moved to London, Tristan went travelling and they didn't see each other for nearly six months. During this time Anna did not waste her time. She studied hard at her course but she also enjoyed life, for the first time out of the world familiar to her. She was experimenting, often in the sense that she was sleeping with other men. Anna knew that after she married Tristan, and whoever she might set her eyes on later, she would be able to be with men from a very small and enclosed social group. In London she could spend a night with a nightclub security guard, with a cab driver or a builder, all of whom she would treat like a social experiment rather than anything else. In all those cases she refused to exchange phone numbers with them and after the act itself, she quite expressly told them why she had slept with them. This gave her a feeling of power and of female domination, in a world which, in her eyes, still belonged to men.

Anna's social life was slightly more complex. Amongst other people on her course Anna found a few familiar faces from St Andrews and a few others who shared the same outlook on life...and background. And they created a closed and hermetic group. It was amazing how all those 'rich kids', as many tutors and students called them, were always finding each other in every school or university they went to, forming a tight and impossible-to-penetrate group only a few days after arrival. They would hang out together, told jokes that only they would understand and even dressed in a uniform way. In the law school it was cool to look like they had never brushed their hair and to be as scruffy and grunge-like as possible. After entering the building, situated on the edge of the River Thames with a view of St Paul's, Anna and her friends would always go to a breakout area, without even responding to "Hello" from the people from outside their group. They would sit together chatting or gossiping and from time to time they would laugh very loudly, being heard in the most remote rooms of the building. Students from outside the group, who would sit in close proximity, would often stand up from their seats and move to other parts of the common room, so intimidating it could be.

In this type of environment Anna felt great. So far in her life she was always surrounded by people similar to her. She had not had much of a chance to exhibit her physical and intellectual attributes in front of people from other walks of life, therefore her social comparison was minimal. In law school with people from all classes, Anna could detect how privileged and advantageous her background was and it made her proud that those less lucky than her could feel the social gap between them. Anna thrived and she was leading the entire group in rudeness against those people who were outside their circle.

On that day, however, things did not work the way she planned. As the results of the exams were published overnight, Anna discovered that one of her scores wasn't what her firm expected her to gain. Thanks to her father's connections, Anna already had a training contract and a big City firm behind her, sponsoring her entire education, providing even the pocket money for her maintenance. They expected her to do well and her current results did not satisfy their requirements. She knew that not only would the firm be disappointed but also her parents who had got used to the fact that Anna had always achieved top grades.

Anna went for a meeting with one of the tutors in order to receive some feedback regarding the exam. The meeting went well but the tutor, despite the pressure she put on him, could not change the grade. She knew what that meant – she would be called by her new employer to explain the situation and Anna hated being told what to do. No one had ever done it and she did not want to change it now.

After the meeting she went to the canteen where the table she had always sat at was occupied by someone else. This situation had happened before and she knew how to deal with it. She would sit by the table, regardless of the person who was already there. Then she would always spread her things gradually, making others squeeze their space. Anna would proceed with this until the situation would be difficult to bear for the other occupiers and they would leave. That happened every time she tried it and she did not see any reason why not to try it again on this occasion.

But the girl in her thick glasses, who Anna had seen only a handful of times before, seemed to not respond to this practice. She visibly did not belong to Anna's world but somehow the girl didn't want to allow Anna to push her into the obvious 'limitations of the social class she belonged to', using Anna's terminology. Anna tried again but the girl did not move a single thing on the table, instead reading something on her phone. Maybe she didn't notice. Maybe she just didn't know who she was dealing with. Anna put her books in the centre of the table and then her pencil case next to it. But the girl, still without raising her head, just moved the books to the other side of the table and put back her stuff, which was all around her. It looked like she was using some technique of resilience, only to annoy Anna. Anna tried again but the situation repeated itself. Anna couldn't tolerate this any longer.

"You seem to be moving my books while I would like to sit here," Anna said with a tone full of confidence.

"It is because you are taking my space. I am happy to

share a table but I would like to keep my things where they are, so you will have to use the space which is available, I am afraid." The girl wasn't disrespectful in the slightest but she was assertive in a way that Anna had never experienced so far.

"I don't think you understand," Anna answered, "this is the table I always sit at and I would like to use it now. So move your stuff so that I can fit in."

"There are many free tables here, so maybe you should take a different table or you can work in the library." The girl was not going to back down.

"Listen, this is my table and I am going to use it, like I always do. And you had better find another spot for yourself. Preferably somewhere where people can't see you."

"Who the hell do you think you are?" The girl was not going to be bossed around. "How can you speak to anyone in this manner? Did your parents not teach you how adult people behave and how they speak to each other? There is a certain manner in which people conduct themselves towards others. I am really surprised that at your age you haven't noticed it yet." The exchange between two women began to catch the attention of other students gathered in the room.

"I always get what I want and I want this table so either you leave or I will make you leave," Anna said through clenched teeth, knowing that it was too late to withdraw.

"Why are you such a vicious little bitch?!" The girl said it very loudly and it could be heard by all the students sitting in the breakout area. Some of them whistled with approval but, to make matters worse, many more started clapping their hands. Anna blushed and immediately looked around in search of her group but none of the rich kids were there and she felt lost.

She picked up her stuff and decided to walk towards the exit. Behind her there was a loud crowd clapping hands with great intensity now. They were all against her and in support of the ugly girl. Anna felt like an outcast. Something was happening which she could not understand. She felt puzzled or – much worse – lost. She could not comprehend the situation. Anna knew that she had to leave the building as soon as it was possible. Forever. She didn't want to see any of those people ever again. Even those from her group, none of them. She was going to go back to her apartment and pack her things. And she would move back to her parents'. She would wait for Tristan there and when he came back she would marry him. Her parents would love the idea of having her with them and Tristan would worship her for their entire life together, only for the favour she did for him by marrying him. These thoughts brought back to Anna a sense of security and stability. She knew where she belonged and why should she care about the world full of riff-raff? She would never meet this mob again in Chipping Norton.

Runaway

He was standing still. In the middle of Alexanderplatz. The crowds were passing him by, running to the nearby station, in order to catch their trains. He could also hear someone playing the piano in the main hall of the railway station. It was one of those pieces from the 'roaring twenties' period which Louis knew well but at this very moment he could not remember the title. The person who played it, somewhere out there, in the shabby and rough departure lobby, wasn't very good at it and Louis felt instantly irritated. He held the phone in his hand next to his ear, as if the conversation with his stepmother was still taking place, although it had finished several seconds before. It started as it usually did:

"Hello, Mum, how are things going?" Louis answered his mobile, seeing her name on the screen.

"Hi, Lu, I wanted to talk about your father." Elisabeth went straight to the point, just like she always did. Being German, she was always very direct and if there was something important to be said, it would be said during the first minutes of the meeting or phone call conversation. No preparations, no tuning up. Just straight to the point, in between the eyes.

Louis had great respect for his stepmother. She had not only brought him up since he was three years old but also stayed faithfully by the side of his father, despite all he did…and said. However, being British, Louis often found it difficult to talk to Elisabeth, even after years of living among Germans. She was very direct, too direct, just like continental Europeans could be. It was something he often found uncomfortable. He always circled around before he said what he wanted to say. She, on the other hand, would express everything that was on her mind without much preparation. It looked like her thoughts were always formed in Germanic-neat shapes of ready-made-perfect phrases. Louis's thoughts were never like that. He had never really known what he thought and sometimes he felt that his brain was endlessly trying to differentiate between what he thought and what he wanted to say. And he would never say what he thought without sieving through it, giving significant consideration to what the others would think of him afterwards.

"John… I mean, your father, had his tests…he is ill, very ill. He has cancer and he needs to start his treatment straight away, without any delay—"

"Mum, wait…wait…please," Louis took a deep breath. The portion of information was greater than he was able to process. And it was about his father. A father who he hadn't seen for seven years.

Louis was brought up as an only child. He was always told, since he was a very little boy, that one day he would take over the company which his father had built over many years of his life. And for a long period of time Louis was willing to do it. To please his father he even graduated in economics. This education was supposed to enable him to manage the family businesses, as by the time he was twenty-one his father's company had grown to a size that no one could have predicted before. It was a mini-empire under Louis's father's strong hand. The problem was that as Louis grew older he had an increasing amount of doubt regarding whether he would like to work in the business at all. Running his father's companies, in particular, was a job he didn't want. Louis had also hated his studies, although he graduated in order to please everyone around him. Then he had started to work in his father's offices, in the room adjacent to his father's.

Louis's family always wanted to control what he was doing and his dad was the most controlling of them all. Louis would have to report to his father twice a day and to communicate all his new ideas and observations about the working system to him or just to brief him on his current activities. Louis also had his own personal assistant. The only other person who had this privilege in the strictly run company was his father. Many managers looked at Louis with anger and frustration as he was given more than they have ever been. Despite the fact that others worked for John for all their lives, influencing the development of the company, Louis was the one who got quick promotions and pay rises without even asking for them. And it did not make him a popular member of staff.

Gradually Louis felt exhausted by the work routines and by the hostility and the competition around him. The most irritating was that by then he already knew what his calling really was. Or at least what he hoped that his calling could be.

Until the age of seventeen Louis had been a keen horse rider. The horses and everything even remotely connected to the equestrian lifestyle were his genuine passion. But three days before his eighteenth birthday he went for a ride which became the last ride of his life. His favourite horse, Benny, got scared of a car speeding by the side of the paddock and threw

Louis off, to the ground, stamping on Louis's unconscious body several times afterwards. Louis ended up in intensive care and was in recovery for nearly a year. Although he managed to get back to almost full health, as a result of back injuries he could never sit on the horse again.

After the accident Louis had felt very down and struggled to see any colour in the world surrounding him. He lost his passion and there was nothing which made sense to him anymore. Louis also had to act in front of his father and to pretend that he coped well with his pain and the physiotherapy. That was the necessity of the situation and reflected the dynamics of the father-son relationship they had both established.

As a child, Louis was never allowed to take a day off from school, even when seriously sick. As a result, once, at the age of eight, Louis ended up in hospital with salmonella, which his father misdiagnosed as an insignificant indigestion. His father was tough himself and he expected everyone else to have the same attitude and self-discipline towards life. He was often criticizing people who were ill or disabled and Louis knew that he should not count on any sympathy from him.

However, Louis's stepmother noticed very quickly how upset and miserable he was after the accident. Louis never had to act in front of Elisabeth. Being from a different country and culture, she seemed to be more understanding of human nature and observant of people's emotions than his father could have ever learned to be. She could always see through Louis, noticing every sad or happy thought or feeling. Elisabeth could also see Louis's strengths and she tried to help him to enhance them, regardless of what that would mean 'for the family'. His father could only see Louis's weaknesses and he recommended 'working on them in the endless process of self-improvement', as he always put it.

Louis was still in the hospital, in pain after yet another leg surgery, when Elisabeth brought him a gift. A camera. It wasn't just a cheap, common-amongst-tourists type of camera but a Nikon D800, which was used by professional photographers. Initially, he thought that this wasn't a good idea on her part. He had no interest in art, at this point, and somehow he could not imagine himself spending any time taking pictures of others. But after a week of lying in the hospital bed, in the same pose and with only his stepmother visiting, Louis was bored. One day he looked at the unpacked camera box resting on his bedside table and thought that he should give it a go. Louis didn't know how to use it in the correct manner though and after a few unsuccessful attempts at taking a decent picture, he put it back where it was. Impatient and angry with himself and his situation, he had fallen asleep.

On the following day, however, he picked up the camera one more time and worked on it, with the instructions, step by step, for hours until he understood how to set the basic functions. And it happened – he took his first good picture. He didn't like it initially but he took one more and then, yet another. In the days, weeks, and months to come he would shoot pictures of pretty nurses, then of the ugly ones, the doctors and the view from the window, as he could see it, in his horizontal position. He would even take pictures of cream-coloured hospital walls. He also began to play with them by zooming in, adding shades and changing the light. And the entire process brought him an amazing amount of joy. Louis knew how it was to be happy again. He felt that he found a purpose in life and a hope and that everything had started to fall in the right place. He was full of energy and was recovering faster than predicted. Even the hospital food seemed to not bother him anymore. Louis could see sense in the world and his life and everything he was putting his hands to, gained a new meaning.

During the weekends Louis's father visited the hospital with his stepmother and Louis knew that he should not show the camera to him. His stepmother had never made any request to keep the gift to himself but somehow Louis's instinct was telling him to hide the camera during those visits. So father was completely unaware of Louis's new passion and the stepmother joined the pact of silence despite the fact that Louis and she had never discussed it between them.

From that time, the camera would accompany Louis everywhere: on his country trekking trips, during his foreign journeys and, especially, during his gap year in China. A year to which his father did not want to agree but, thanks to the help of his stepmother and his grandmother, Louis managed to obtain his consent. He was taking pictures every hour of the day and he was very proud of them. One of them was sent by Elisabeth to a contest where Louis, only twenty years old then, had won third prize. At that point of his life the passion he established for photography did not seem to be sufficiently strong to him to pursue it as a profession. It was only a hobby. Louis also knew that it would not be possible to have this sort of career as his father would hate the idea of any artistic future for his only son.

John seemed to know that his son had other activities aside from school and university but he never really asked. And as Louis had very high grades and received only positive comments from his teachers, his father seemed to decide to allow him to do with his spare time whatever he wanted, following the rule: 'Don't ask, don't tell'.

At the age of twenty-six and after working for three years, side by side with his father, Louis felt that he would much rather die than carry on this way any longer. He knew that he had to do something to change his life before it was too late and before he would lose all the energy to do it. And, deep down, he hoped that life could be more about him realizing his desires and passions; he hoped that photography could become something more than just a spare-time activity. He wanted it to be his full-time occupation. Even if it was badly paid, it would be done with devotion and determination.

In January, during a dinner celebrating his twenty-seventh birthday in the newly refurbished Hilton Hotel restaurant overlooking Park Lane and Hyde Park, Louis announced his intention to travel to Berlin for a month. Berlin seemed to be the easiest option. Due to his stepmother's connections he had visited Berlin often during his young life and there were many of her relatives there who could and would help him. Louis's German was very basic and mostly forgotten since his secondary school days but he knew he would have some people to rely on in Berlin, in case things went badly. That was already something. He could start a new life without supervision and pressure.

From the very beginning Louis intended not to come back. His plan was not to ever live in the same town or even in the same country as his father. He also knew that the only way to share this piece of information with his father would be to tell him about it from there, from Berlin or wherever he would be by then. Louis couldn't tell his father the truth in person, face to face. He was always petrified of John and he knew that his strong opposition to his son's plans could take away from Louis any courage he had managed to accumulate.

At the dinner, during the conversation about the German trip John did not express much interest. He only wanted to know how Louis was going to organize his workload during his absence and whether he had filled in a holiday form. His stepmother looked at Louis suspiciously. Although they were not related biologically, they had always had a bond which allowed them to communicate without words.

After the dinner, while they were waiting for a taxi outside the hotel and John was smoking round the corner, Elisabeth whispered in Louis's ear,

"What will be your permanent address in Berlin?"

Louis looked at her and blushed. They both smiled at each other,

"I don't know yet. I was thinking of renting a small flat somewhere. At least for as long as the money lasts..."

"Don't waste the money. I will give you the address of one of my cousins. She has an apartment on Bulow Strasse. She is an aging spinster and has many odd habits but she will be happy to take you. It is not the nicest part of town but you will be sitting conveniently, having within easy reach Potsdamer Platz on one side and Ku'damm on the other side. I will call her tonight."

Louis felt his eyes filling with tears although he didn't want to cry. He felt free. There was eventually something to look forward to. He liked Berlin with its scruffiness of old nineteenth century apartment houses, mixed with the new and minimalistic glass buildings. He also loved the fact that this town, despite its long history, was still very visibly not shaped. Big plots of land left as demarcation zones between East and West Berlin were vigorously filled with the new designs of the streets unseen since the World War Two. Berlin had a vibe, class and was not as ostentatious and pushy as London. He could get lost there, making himself known only to those he wanted to see. And more importantly it was far enough from London to have a life without being overlooked and controlled.

He remembered, like it was today, his arrival and the first day in Berlin. It was the first day of his independent, adult life. From the airport he took a train to Alexanderplatz and from there the tube to Bulow Strasse. Later he would walk from there to many places but on that day Berlin seemed to be all new to him and he wanted to keep it that way. And the newcomers always used public transport.

Despite having been in Berlin many times before, Louis felt on that day that it was a completely different town. It was a place which was supposed to be his home and he looked at it through the perspective of his new life, starting on that day. After leaving the luggage in the apartment of Elisabeth's cousin he went straight to see some of the sights of the town. He wanted to see them now like they were the sights of his hometown, which Berlin became. After walking around the old centre he sat down in a little café in the Unter den Linden and had a big, proper breakfast. Then he walked to Adlon where he ordered a coffee and a slice of cake which he consumed in their lobby, listening to the calming sound of the fountain. He did it all at once, with a very short time between breakfast and the cake. Louis wanted to experience and to remember as much as he could from that day, as everything was so different, despite being so familiar. And he liked how different it all felt.

Since then, he managed not only to pursue his dream career but he also achieved some considerable success. By now his works were exhibited everywhere from Hamburg to New York and his pictures had found their way onto the covers of well-known magazines. With the recognition, the financial success came and Louis had not only a fashionable loft apartment in Kreuzberg but also a house in Dordogne where he often drove to after a few busy weeks of socializing and networking in Berlin. His name was not anonymous anymore but more importantly his style of photography, so individual and emotional, was recognizable enough to create high demand for his work. And during all those years Louis not only did not cease to enjoy taking pictures but he was passionate about the photography even more than when he started. Taking pictures brought to Louis a fulfilment and a sense of belonging. Because he was belonging to his art.

However, his success did not come without a high price. A week after he moved to Berlin he called home. His father answered the phone – he always did and when occasionally his stepmother picked it up, it was so unusual that everybody asked whether her husband was alright.

"Hello, Dad, how are you?" Louis asked.

"I am very good, thank you. And how are you, Louis? How is Berlin?" his father reciprocated.

"I am really well. Berlin is very vibrant but at the same time extremely relaxing. They built several new buildings at the back of Potsdamerstrasse. You should see them, Dad. You would really like them..."

"I suppose you did not call me to talk about the

architecture, Louis. When are you coming back? I need you at work. I understand that sometimes young people need to have some time off and I did not ask what you are doing there but it is high time for you to come back. I spent all my life working hard for you and now, when the businesses are growing, I cannot be left on my own doing all of this. I did not tell you this before but I think it was a very selfish decision to leave me behind with all this on my shoulders..."

"Dad, I am sorry that you feel that way, but I do not think you worked for all these years just for me..."

"When your mother left us..."

"Dad, she didn't leave us. She left you and she left me with you, because she suffered from depression and she couldn't look after me..."

"Is that the fairy tale she is spreading now? Very interesting but it is all nonsense. She left us and we were on our own and I looked after you all your life and you owe me something now..."

"I do not owe you anything, Dad!" Louis said it loud and there was a silence on the phone. "Dad, you have to understand that whatever happened between you and Tonia," Louis always called his biological mother by her first name, "it was between you two. And yes, you did bring me up but all parents bring their children up. It is not a favour one does but a part of our lives and we cannot expect anything in exchange for doing this—"

"I am not used to being preached at by people who don't have a clue what they are talking about," his father interrupted, "and I am not going to be taught by someone who doesn't even have his own children, someone who achieved nothing. Someone who relies on everything from his family..."

"I do not rely on my family for anything! You made me to stay, to be there under your sight so that you could control me. I couldn't even go to university outside of London."

"UCL is one of the top universities in the country and I don't see why I should pay for anything outside of London, if you could have studied here...and to live at home which cost much less."

"Do you really think that it was about the money and the standard of the university, Dad? Or maybe about having me by your side, so that I could do what you wanted me to do and be who you wanted me to be."

"Louis, I think this conversation has gone too far. I need to know when you are back for our human resources department. I don't want people to talk behind my back that you have special treatment, just like you always do."

"I am not coming back, Dad..."

The silence on the phone lasted for several seconds this time. Louis knew that his father was furious and that he was thinking about some sharp response or maybe Louis expected this because that was how his father always behaved. But the tone of the next sentence was different:

"So, you are leaving me without taking any responsibility... Your mother did the same years ago and look at her life now!"

"She is perfectly happy, Dad, though I do not remember whether I have ever seen you happy..."

"You always know best!" his father shouted now. "If I knew I was going to bring up such a selfish twat as you I wouldn't have bothered. I should have pursued my life ambitions instead of sacrificing everything for you. You have destroyed my life, just like your mother did!"

"You have destroyed your life yourself because you use people for your own goals, because you want to own everyone and everything!"

"I have had enough of this conversation! I will watch you falling! You will come back one day but then my terms will be very different."

"Dad, you are my father, you cannot say things like that. I would like you to be a part of my life. But it would be my life which means the life I will choose for myself…"

"I am not interested in the misery you are going to live. You have no money and you will not inherit anything after my death. I will make sure you will not."

"I will be fine, Dad," Louis responded with resignation. This conversation had gone in a direction he never wanted it to go.

"You know, many years ago, your mother had a similar conversation with me when she left. She was also supposed to be fine. And somehow she wasn't. Her numerous marriages and divorces say everything really, don't you think?" Louis's father seemed to be pleased with any pain which his first wife might have experienced during her life.

"At least she lived her life, Dad, and she wasn't making others live theirs in her way. She was just trying her best," Louis interrupted yet another monologue of his father.

"If your mummy is so fantastic then leave me alone and fuck off to her!" his father put the phone down.

Louis did not try to call him back. He really felt that he had had enough. The relationship with his father over the years washed Louis of many emotions and killed most of the warm feelings he had ever had towards him. And this last conversation brought peace into Louis's life. He suddenly discovered that life without his father meant life without an everlasting burden. He felt young and fresh and enjoyed every moment of his independence.

Since the conversation with his father, Louis rang home only a handful of times. Each time when his father answered the phone, he passed the phone straight to Elisabeth. Louis didn't want to apologize but he knew that he had to. However, all those attempts were dismissed and his father didn't want to talk to him. He even didn't call Louis for his thirtieth birthday.

But over the next few years Louis learnt to live without his father and he genuinely did not miss him. The love wasn't there anymore and even the sense of duty became less pronounced. Louis had regular contact with other members of his family, who all tried to help heal their relationship. But John seemed not to be interested and Louis simply gave up.

The phone call from Elisabeth, answered at the Alexanderplatz, came out of nowhere. The thought that his father may be dying, that he may be dead anytime, did not bring any emotion to Louis. In a cold and rational manner he felt that the death of his father could be a final closure: the end of a chapter which should have ended a long time ago.

Louis started walking towards the Unter den Linden. He walked for a few minutes until he reached the Berliner Dom and a huge building site, where hundreds of builders were rebuilding the Imperial Castle or rather its modern-day version. Thoughts were rumbling in his head and he didn't know what to do. On one hand he felt he should go to London in order to see his father. On the other he thought about a trip to South Africa, which he was supposed to undertake the following day. He felt torn. Initially he wanted to go to

London but then he thought that there was no point going there now. If his father was going to have treatment and he was told only recently about the illness, it would be very difficult to have any civilized conversation between the two of them. And the illness would only put an additional strain on their relationship. And if he was going to die? John had already been dead to Louis for the past seven years. What would it change to see him again and to have yet another pointless argument? Louis decided. He did not want to see his father. Not after all the years when John was humiliating and dominating him. And not after the last seven years when Louis's father did not show any interest in his life. Louis didn't want to see him and he didn't want to open the door that he felt had been closed for too long.

He was going to call his stepmother the following morning and tell her he was not coming. Not now, not ever. Louis and Elisabeth could always meet, as they used to before, in the various European cities, with or without his father's knowledge. And they could talk then. She could always keep him updated about his father's condition but Louis didn't want to see his father again. Ever.

Louis knew he would feel guilty about his decision but he didn't know that this guilt would follow him for the rest of his life. He also didn't know that this guilt would turn him into another, more miserable, version of his father. But on that day he felt light and happy. He took a deep breath and caught a taxi, which took him to Ku'damm. He desperately needed to buy new swimwear for his Cape Town trip.

The Last Journey

The sun was shining with a massive strength and the plane was coming down to land. I have always loved this moment, when a plane was about to land at this airport. The sea below the plane was incredibly blue. It seemed to wrap the entire town up so that it looked like Nice wasn't on a coast but on a big island surrounded by endless waters. This view has always been very beautiful, although on that day it was even more astonishing than ever before. All the waters beneath were reflecting the yellow-gold colour of the sun and the entire view from our little windows was incredibly radiant. The inside of the plane was very bright as well and most of the passengers had to keep their eyes closed, being blinded by the reflections. It was surreal and serene. But the beauty of the moment might have been emphasized by the circumstances of my trip. I knew it was my last visit and I came to say goodbye. I was dying and I wanted for the last time to put my foot on the only place which was a home to me.

I came to the Cote d'Azur for the first time as a young boy. We started our visit from Nice. Back then, in the early sixties, the town was still full of its pre-war glory, although parts were already taken slowly by the mass immigration which nearly destroyed this place in the seventies. I remember when my dad took my hand and walked me from the ship we arrived on. The bridge was very narrow and I was scared. The harbour did not look pretty but was very exotic. Sailors of all colours were sitting lazily, smoking cigarettes or drinking beer by the sea, waiting for their boats to leave. From there we took a taxi and went to our hotel. Through the windows of the car I watched with fascination the vibrant crowds on the streets and in the markets. The colourful marquees were spread above the café gardens and restaurant windows providing shelter from the sun to people having their morning coffee and croissants. We were driven alongside the Promenade des Anglais and my dad opened a window, saying, "Look at the waves crashing on the shore. You will never find sea more beautiful anywhere in the world." And my father knew what he was saying. Brought up in a French family in the colonies of North Africa, he'd put his foot on all continents and now wanted to show to his only child the beloved Old World. I can recall the intensity of the colours and smells of this first visit, although it gets confused with so many more which came later, during the years which followed.

I fell in love with Nice from the very first sight. Its baroque architecture, its decadent boulevards and narrow and rather rough streets seemed instantly fascinating to me as a little boy. This fascination stayed with me until today, despite all the later experiences. In Nice I always feel as happy as I was at the age of twelve.

I went through customs and took a left to the taxi station. Then, halfway through, I realized that I didn't want to take a cab this time. I wanted to walk all the way from the airport, alongside the beach to the old town, where I was staying. I was going to spend only one night in Nice and on the following day I was heading to Cannes where I had a flat. In the left pocket of my trousers I had two little keys to the apartment of Belinda, my friend from London who had offered it to me to use during this trip. Belinda bought this spacious pad a few years back using the inheritance from her mother, and treated it like the biggest treasure she had ever had. It was a privilege to be offered the place as she hardly ever lent it to anyone. And she didn't even know about the reason for this last-minute escapade.

After an hour or so walking I got to the place. It was just behind the opera house, at Rue Raul Bosio, in my favourite part of the Old Town. I climbed the stairs of the eighteenth-century palazzo and opened the door to the apartment. Its luxurious interior was quite overwhelming and as soon as I'd dropped my luggage off I left for a late lunch. I sat down at the Place du Palace de Justice, in the same restaurant as always. I used to come to this place with my dad nearly half of a century ago. Later I used to come here on my own, with various girlfriends and with those three of them who later became my wives too. I also brought my daughter here just after her eighteenth birthday. The interior had hardly changed, only the faces of the waiters were different. The old owner, Jean-Luc, must have died years ago. His small figure with a big belly was the main culinary attraction of the square for many decades until he just wasn't there anymore. At the moment the restaurant was more airy than before and was being run by a group of very good-looking Italians. The food has never been the strength of the place but the location was. Whether you had lunch, dinner or just a coffee, you could see the flowing crowds of people of all races, colours and nationalities. There was only one thing they all had in common: they had this easy walk, the type of which people who are on holiday have. Without any rush or sense of urgency. I have always liked coming here, having coffee and just watching the street passing.

Two hours later I went back to the apartment in order to have a short nap and to get changed before the evening. I was going to the opera that night with my old friend François and his new wife, Odile. From what I heard last year, François, who was in his late sixties, married one of his students, who – I believe – only recently got her right to vote. Typical story, I thought – intellectual fascination of a young and pretty girl with extremely clever heavily middle-aged mathematician. Life loves repeatable scripts.

I woke up at a quarter to seven, far later than I had planned. I was sleeping on the daybed in the high-ceiling drawing room, crowned with an amazing crystal chandelier hanging above. All the furniture was very stylish, maybe even too stylish. I got up and walked towards the little black Chinese cabinet from where I took a big glass and half filled it with cognac. Yes, it was too much. And I wasn't a drunk but my afternoon nap left me with a certain level of anxiety. The anxiety which I have always felt when I allowed myself to relax and let the concerns go. Maybe that is why I became a writer. I could cure my worries by passing them onto my fictional characters.

I went to the modern bathroom and walked into the shower covered behind a big see-through glass wall. Warm water was pouring down my body. I still am fit, I thought, looking down at my chest and hips. I have exercised all my life and did yoga even in the days when it was still mostly considered to be an activity of lefties and intellectual junkies.

I looked at least ten years younger but somehow my good physique wasn't compatible with what was underneath. And that part of me decided to abort this world. Why not any of those fat people walking on the streets? Why not one of those ugly ones? Or even better: why not someone stupid instead? I laughed at the inappropriate thoughts that crossed my mind. I didn't feel guilty. Those were just reasonable questions of a person who did not have to be concerned anymore by any political correctness and who was ready to go. Or was I? I have never known whether my sarcasm and irony were a sign of intelligence and a healthy distance and resignation towards what is in life unavoidable, or maybe it was an outlet for the inside cruelty and darkness. The water was burning me. I turned the shower off and wrapped myself in a large thick white towel. I went back to the drawing room and poured myself another glass of cognac. I needed it desperately. Even if I came across as tipsy that night, François and Odile would never see me again. What did it matter in those circumstances?

I got dressed in my dinner jacket brought from London and went to the kitchen to make myself a coffee. I needed something to put me back firmly on my feet. I wasn't sure whether I suddenly felt weak as a result of the alcohol I drank and the empty stomach or was it my illness kicking in. The coffee did help and at quarter past seven I went down the stairs and crossed the road to the opera building. Its noble façade was very moderately lit and a group of people were standing in front of it. I recognized François and waved. He didn't notice me. He and a younger woman, probably Odile, seemed to be having an argument. And it was a very French argument, full of gesticulation and with both parties walking off every few seconds.

Suddenly François noticed me and his big fat face smiled. He was now walking towards me and had both his arms widely spread. We embraced and kissed on both cheeks.

"It so good to see you, Paul!" he shouted. "So good! Really fantastic…" He was talking all the time. He always was. He even argued with himself and one didn't have to interject much into conversations. "I want to introduce you to my wife…"

As we came closer, I realized that Odile wasn't beautiful. Not even pretty. Rather short and with thick glasses, she reminded me of boy from my school in Vienna who was a favourite pupil of the history teacher. He was very eager to provide an answer to her every question and this knowledge seemed to compensate for everything that was regrettable about his looks. Odile was just the same – ugly, with a rather bad complexion, she seemed to be very keen.

"Hello, Mr de Pervieux, I am Odile," she said showing me a big smile of yellow teeth.

"What Mr de Pervieux?! What Mr de Pervieux?!" François shouted. "It is Paul! My very good friend and stop making me uncomfortable, how young you are!" he said to Odile, and then added to both of us, "The price of being with an old man is to speak to many other old people by using their first names." He was smiling and it was visible that she made him really happy and proud. While saying this he was also patting my left shoulder, which started to hurt as a result.

"But it is not a matter of age! I cannot call a famous author by his first name!" Odile responded. She was very agitated and it looked like they were about to argue.

"It is very nice to meet you," I interrupted them and smiled broadly. "I have heard a lot about you." I thought that a good lie made awkward situations more bearable. "And yes, please call me Paul."

"I am honoured, Mr...I mean, Paul. I really am a great fan of your books and when François told me you know each other, I couldn't believe him..."

"In fact she still didn't believe me when we were walking here to meet up with you," François added.

"It is really good to see you, my old friend, and to see you so happy," I said to François, ignoring for a second his chatty new wife. "We haven't seen each other for at least five, maybe six years..."

"Eight, exactly eight years in March!" François corrected me, "It was in San Francisco and I was staying with you and your wife...then-wife, I meant." François blushed.

"I didn't know you live in San Francisco," Odile interrupted. "I have always wanted to visit the West Coast"

"I did. I don't anymore. After our divorce my ex-wife kept the house and I re-located to London to be close to my daughter. She was doing her degree in England and I wanted to see more of her..."

"How is Isabelle?" François asked, which was quite strange considering he actually never met her.

"She is doing very well. She works as a designer and as soon as she graduated, she moved to New York where she has been working for a fashion house. So again we are living on two different continents... Anyway, enough of me boring you with the history of my life. Let's go in – we have only ten minutes until the start and I am desperate for a drink," and we walked towards the building.

A Brahms piano concerto was playing in the Opera House that night and I liked piano concertos. The thought of listening to Brahms in a beautiful opera building in Nice, just several metres from the sea, put me in an excellent mood. I felt relaxed like I hadn't in months, though the idea that it may be my last time was slightly spoiling the perfection of the moment. The other element which was slipping in and ruining the situation was the fact that the interval was unavoidable and that I would have to make conversation with François and his wife. I missed François and, although I didn't mind Odile, somehow I felt that my last moments should be spent with people I wanted to be with and Odile wasn't one of them. Before the beginning of the concert we were in the bar ordering champagne to our box and Odile was pouring on me her knowledge of my books and her understanding of my characters. It did flatter me but I simply didn't want to talk about them. Not now, at least. I was hoping that François and I would have a chance to talk and I knew, by then, that with Odile's fascination with my books and...me, we would struggle to talk at all.

The concert was played in a magnificent way – the Russian female pianist hit every note with such a passion that one could forget about the entire world. While she was playing, she was moving her body in accordance with the sounds she was making so that it looked like she was at a rock concert, not a classical music one. Her shapes were very unusual too: she was incredibly fat but with no breasts and her weight came as a contrast to the lightness and easiness with which she was playing.

I looked towards François. He wasn't really listening. His head was turned towards Odile and she was looking back at him. They held their hands and were smiling at each other, just like two teenagers who had fallen in love for the first time. I felt jealous about their experience. I never felt this way. Maybe because I had always been with women who resembled my personality and background too much. Brought up in an old noble family with great pride but very little money, I felt only comfortable with women of old breeding such as myself. They were intelligent, sharp, skinny and elegant. Every single one of them. But sadly none of them had the emotional weight I, deep down, was eager to get from them. All my relationships were mostly concentrated on sex and this purely biological act was fulfilling every liaison. After a while, when the satisfaction was replaced by boredom, I would move swiftly to another one, starting yet again from the beginning. But there might have been another reason why all of them ended in the same way and why for the last three years I have decided to stay on my own, despite that there were still many women interested in me, such as Belinda. Maybe it was me. Maybe my shallowness, selfishness, my inability to build anything more meaningful caused it. Wasn't that the reason why my daughter was running away from me, emotionally and geographically, as soon as I managed to get closer to her? Wasn't that the reason why I became an author? So that I could dive into my inner feelings daily, satisfying the deep need of emotional masturbation and having a justification that I have to do it for a living. Or maybe I was too harsh on myself. And maybe this element of my personality damaged all my relationships. Maybe I was never happy with myself and worked harder and harder instead of…living my life and enjoying the day. I really must be dying, I thought, and laughed quietly.

The concert finished and we all left the building, me and François first with Odile following behind. The first moment out of the building was like an injection of life. The fresh sea air smacked our faces with gentleness. It was revitalizing and stood in contrast with the heavy and stuffy interior of the Opera House. Suddenly I felt in a splendid mood and suggested a walk across town. Though this practice was never very safe in the Old Town of Nice, it was always one of my favourite things to do. François and Odile agreed though one could see that the only thing they really wanted to do was to go home and have sex. I wasn't angry with François, despite the initial irritation. I didn't tell him about my reason for visiting and he obviously treated my stay as just one of many visits. Not understanding the gravity of my position, he simply enjoyed himself. And although I had intended to tell him that night about my illness, I decided against it. There was no point spoiling his good time; he quite obviously had his five minutes of happiness and maybe it was better for him to memorize me the way I was: still good looking and a winner. After all to others I was a best-selling author, who spent his life in relationships with the most beautiful women. A happy father of a very clever daughter whose life, and one could already see it, was going to be a straight path to success. One could tell that not only by the career she already had, despite the young age, but also by the look of her husband, equally carefully brought up and the heir to a real estate empire himself. Isabelle had managed to change all the weaknesses of an old-fashioned and stiff European upbringing into a social success on the other side of the Atlantic, where this sort of behaviour had an allure of sweetness of the good old continent and was considered very aristocratic. With me it always was different – in so many ways I was trapped in between worlds, not knowing which one to choose and as a result not fitting into any of them. But people didn't have to know about the other, well-hidden, side of my life. About the feeling of loneliness and intellectual isolation. About the persistent angst, cured by far too many antidepressants. And this part of me should die with me so that people could see only what was good in me till the end. Just like they could only see my well-shaped body, not knowing about the disgusting cancer eating everything that was inside of it.

We said goodbye to each other in the harbour from where they intended to take a taxi home while I decided to walk for a bit longer. The last words we said to each other were, on their side, full of a genuine hope that we will meet soon. On my side, it was different. I was trying to memorize as much as I could have from the last minute I saw the face of François: our last shake of hands, my last touch of his skin. The last words which my friend of over half of the century was telling me. I did everything to make it easy or at least everything to make it *look* easy for them.

An hour later I was back in the apartment. I was standing in the big French window with another glass full of cognac watching the street sweepers and the odd lost tourist. I wasn't sad. I was looking forward to the next day and to those several more during which I was going to enjoy the most spectacular sights the world has to offer. And they all will be mine because only I will understand the importance of them to me, the significance of the entire journey.

The following morning I walked towards the station from where I took a train to Cannes. I longed to see my old little studio flat and I couldn't wait to sit on my tiny balcony overlooking the steep Rue de Saint-Antoine. I was so eager and excited like it was my first trip there, not the last one. Or maybe it was my first journey. The first journey to understand myself, the first journey to a new and satisfied me. And it didn't matter how long it would last. This first journey was something worth living and...dying.